BEYOND SILENCE

BOOKS BY ELEANOR CAMERON

The Mushroom Planet Books
The Wonderful Flight to the Mushroom Planet
Stowaway to the Mushroom Planet
Mr. Bass's Planetoid
A Mystery for Mr. Bass
Time and Mr. Bass

Other Books for Young People
The Terrible Churnadryne
The Mysterious Christmas Shell
The Beast with the Magical Horn
A Spell Is Cast
A Room Made of Windows
The Court of the Stone Children
To the Green Mountains
Julia and the Hand of God
Beyond Silence

Novel
The Unheard Music

Essays
The Green and Burning Tree: On the Writing
and Enjoyment of Children's Books

BEYOND SILENCE

Eleanor Cameron

E. P. DUTTON   NEW YORK

The lines on the facing page quoted from Loren Eiseley's
work are reprinted by permission of Mabel L. Eiseley,
Executrix of the Estate of Loren C. Eiseley.

The lines on page 88 from "The Song of Shadows" are
reprinted by permission of The Literary Trustees of
Walter de la Mare and The Society of Authors as their
representative. "The Song of Shadows" is from *Peacock Pie*
by Walter de la Mare. Copyright © 1961
by Alfred A. Knopf, Inc.

Library of Congress Cataloging in Publication Data

Cameron, Eleanor, date   Beyond silence.

Summary: Troubled by a recurring nightmare following
his brother's death, Andrew accompanies his father
to the family castle in Scotland where he has several
encounters with one of his forebears.
[1. Death—Fiction. 2. Space and time—Fiction.
3. Scotland—Fiction] I. Title.
PZ7.C143Be 1980 [Fic] 80-10350 ISBN: 0-525-26463-9

Published in the United States by E. P. Dutton, a Division
of Elsevier-Dutton Publishing Company, Inc., New York

Published simultaneously in Canada by Clarke,
Irwin & Company Limited, Toronto and Vancouver

Editor: Ann Durell   Designer: Claire Counihan

Printed in the U.S.A.   First Edition
10 9 8 7 6 5 4 3 2 1

The universe begins to look more like a
great thought than like a great machine.
                              —Sir James Jeans

Nature contains that which has no intention
of taking us into its confidence.
                              —Loren Eiseley

The future enters into us, in order to
transform itself in us, long before it happens.
                              —Rainer Maria Rilke

CHAPTER

I

Late gray afternoon with a fierce wind whipping down the loch, driving spots of rain against the windshield—no, windscreen it is in Scotland. Then my father's voice, "And here I'd wanted it to be magnificent when you first saw it, Andy. The way I've seen it so many times." But *he* wasn't disappointed. He was home, and only trying to keep himself reined in, because after all he was over forty, but emotional, that kind of Scot. And it was the Celt in him, my mother would say, that made him intense, like the Welsh and the Irish. Any crisis he took full force, like her refusal to go on this journey.

He was sitting up front in the old yellow van with Jim McBride, the man who owned Cames now and had turned it into a hotel, and would twist his head a little to toss remarks back to me, but all the time looking, feasting, I could see, the way his big shoulders continually shifted from side to side and his head went back and forth while he was trying to take in everything at once: his own part of Scotland again for the first time since leaving for America at the age of twenty.

As for me, I can still remember distinctly, six years later, how the sun all at once pierced between two masses of clouds and sent a shaft of radiance along the gray, moving surface of the loch, turning it glinting and metallic where the light fell. At once, everything changed. The green of the trees along the far shore seemed to take on depth but at the same time brilliance and clarity of detail, and the houses over there, scattered along by the water, stood out suddenly with such jewel-like sharpness that each took on a minute character of its own.

"By God, Andy—just when I said I wanted it to be magnificent."

Hoagy should be here, I thought. Any other way never even thought of. But no use thinking. Just take everything for now, for the moment. Don't go outside it or back. Don't go back.

"Now" was the end of that interminable flight from California to London, and following our stay in London, the train journey up through England and Scotland—finally, after all the years Dad had been telling me about the castle ever since I was three or four, the would-be castle on the shore of the loch.

"Nothing's any different, Andy—all exactly as it was. Maybe a few more houses along in here, but really the same—"

We swung around a corner, the loch road so narrow that passing cars all but scraped us, and I sucked in my breath and my sides seemed to shrink, but Jim hardly let up on the throttle, hurtling around bends as if we were in the middle of a freeway.

"Now, here we go, young man. Roll down the window on the right—"

"There it is! There—do you see it?" Dad might have been ten, or maybe twelve, but of course he *was* ten or twelve again, rounding this curve where he'd always gotten his first glimpse of the castle after waiting for nine months at home in the city, filled with all his blissful memories of the summer before.

I rolled down the window and put my head into the wind.

It stood high up, built of the warm, pinkish brown stone of the countryside, turned coppery in the last, rich light of the sun against the black sky. Flags flew from its turrets; chimneys and abutments lifted out of the surrounding greenery above the loch, and the green hills rolled away and away behind it. (I'd climb those hills; I'd have almost four weeks to explore, and I wanted to go alone.) There it was, all lighted up, then lost, then glimpsed again, and lost, as the road curved by the lochside.

He used to run along here when he was a boy, Dad said, back and forth the three miles to the pier during vacations, and all the cousins would gather and race up and down the stairs at the castle right to the top story, then around and around inside the turrets, playing hide-and-seek inside the giant wardrobes, under the massive beds, shouting and making an ungodly racket, he supposed, but no one seemed to mind, old Aunt Millicent least of all, who'd been in her seventies even then.

"And I remember the baths, Jim. I wonder if any of them are still there. They were wooden— mahogany—and zinc inside, of course, and they had hoods. Why the hoods, d'you suppose? Maybe to keep off drafts. And they must have weighed a ton, those things. The maids would bring up water in buckets, because any sort of plumbing for upstairs, when I was a boy, wasn't even thought of."

"There's still one left," said Jim. "The only moveable one now, and it's in the Quark's room. He always insists on having the same room each summer for the same length of time, and having the bath. Can't imagine why. He never uses it, naturally. He's got a bathroom with a regular tub. Just likes the old one, that's all—says it amuses him. Maybe he sleeps in it."

"The Quark?" I asked.

"One of the summer residents. You'll meet them all, though we don't have many, or at least they come and go. Most of the business is dinner, evenings. People come from around, even from the other side of the loch, for Beth's cooking."

Now a wall of the same pinkish stone as the castle began running along on the right and, as the van swayed in at an opening, Jim ground into second and we went racketing up a winding drive cut deep into the hillside where branches leaned in a tangle over walls that rose over our heads ten or fifteen feet on either side, then lessened in height near the top. The walls were cushioned with moss, bright emerald, that looked as if it had been rained on for weeks. Out we came into the open, swerved, drew into the courtyard, "And here you are," said Jim, "and welcome to ye both."

I got out and stood leaning into the wind at the back of the van to get my bags and carry them in. I looked up at the castle, not hearing what the other two were saying, thinking how it was just like its photograph on the folder, yet how you could never begin to imagine a thing or a place as it would actually be—not from a photograph, not outside the experience of it.

But Dad had been right: it *was* enormous, though whether ugly or handsome I couldn't judge. It was just itself, its peculiar, special self, a construction of bays and wings and towers and irregular rooflines, chimneys with figures outlined in the brick, and innumerable windows on confusing levels so that you couldn't begin to imagine how the stairs would go. You had to tilt your head right back to look up at the chimney tops and the pennants cracking in the wind.

I got my bags from Jim and followed Dad up the steps—and the instant I entered the dark hall, took in with a shock, without realizing exactly what I was taking in, the fact that it was shabbily furnished with pieces that bore no relation to one another, that the wallpaper above the blackish brown paneling was ugly (wallpaper in a castle?) and, as I put my bags down, that a long strip of soiled pink drugget (I didn't know then that it was called that) had been laid over the carpet for wet or muddy shoes coming in out of the wild Scottish weather.

So this was Cames, whose interior Dad had described to us time and again as having such elegance. This was his memory of delight! It would have been funny if it hadn't been so sad: to have come all these thousands of miles from Berkeley for this.

Yes, but it was "our" castle, the family castle, built

in the early 1700s by an extremely wealthy Alexander Cames (there've always been Alexanders in the family—Dad is an Alexander—just as there've always been Andrews). However, Dad isn't in the direct line, being a second or third cousin, and when the last of the central Cameses died away, the castle was left to his Great-aunt Millicent. And when she found herself hard up in her nineties, she sold it to the McBrides, packed herself up and went off to live with relatives in Edinburgh, died six months later, and left her money to them. What there was of it. The McBrides were still in debt, running close to the edge, having started this enormous project with very little cash.

So now, in this instant, taking in everything by osmosis after letting go my bags, I saw the short ginger-haired man with thick-lensed glasses, a compact, sturdy man in tweeds and well-shined brogues, leaning against the wall by the big table covered with magazines and travel folders.

He had one foot up behind him, the sole of it pressed against the paneling, and his arms were folded on his chest. He'd been leafing through a magazine as if in utter boredom and had tossed it down with a flick while he studied Dad and then the heavy bag of golf clubs Jim had let slide to the floor. Now our eyes met and he nodded. He nodded slowly, partly in greeting, it might have been, or perhaps in company with his thoughts, then said, smiling, as if amused, "So here we are now, the young master arriving at last." And it sounded to me as if I'd been talked about for weeks, so that Ginger Hair had gotten fed up with it and now was chuckling privately at his first sight of "the young master."

I felt a spurt of anger sharpened by my intense disappointment, but then Dad turned as if to go into the living room—or drawing room, of course, in a castle. "Any mail for us, Jim?" he asked. Yet why would there be, I wondered. We'd stayed several days in London, but even so— "No, no, of course not," Dad caught himself. "It takes eight—seven or eight days, doesn't it?" But it seems so long, is what you mean, I thought, and you want to hear from home but you're horribly afraid you won't, my mother being buried in her new book.

"But there *is* a letter—" began Jim, just as Beth McBride came in, and I couldn't reconcile the two, Jim and his wife. Jim looked like a young D. H. Lawrence with his auburn hair combed straight over and his extremely thin face and deep-set eyes and short auburn beard. But Beth had white hair. She was beautiful; well, perhaps not quite, taken feature by feature, but still, somehow, she struck me as that and always has, with her almost black eyes full of eager interest, and her dark brows and wide mouth and smooth, pale skin.

"Mr. Cames," she said, "Mr. Alexander Cames— welcome at last," she said, stopping on her way to take Dad's hand and shake it. "Welcome to you both," and then came smiling over to me. "Hello, young man." She held out her hands with the letter in one of them, as if she were greeting me again after not more than a year or so, when we'd never met in our lives.

As I took her hands, I felt a kind of immediate recognition passing between us, some instantaneous knowledge that we were drawn to one another, that we'd be in tune with each other and that it would take no time at all for this to happen.

"I'm glad you're here, Andrew. I hope you'll be happy. I have something for you already—what do you think of that?" A glint of mischief kindled her eyes as if she'd been saving this surprise with pleasure. "A letter has come. See here, 'Andrew Durrell Cames, Esquire,' it says. It must be yours, because there is no other Andrew Durrell Cames that I know of can be reached here at the castle." She handed it to me, and I took it and stared at it in complete puzzlement.

The address, small, but clear and precise, with rather rounded letters (a Scottish hand—Dad's is like that) had been written in brown ink, now faded, with a fine pen; a real one, of course, not a ball-point. The pinkish brown stamp was of Queen Victoria. I turned it over and thought it must never have been opened until I ran a fingernail under the edge of the flap. It was scarcely sealed, as if it had been opened and then become lightly stuck down again. It was a fat, cushiony letter and felt, for some reason, right—or rather, satisfying and compact in the palm of my hand. But it had never been sent, I saw when I turned it over and studied the face of it again. At least there was no postmark.

"It can't be mine," I said, holding it out.

"D'ye not want it, then?" Beth exclaimed. Her face was vivid, changing with every emotion. Now it was full of almost comically disappointed surprise. "But it belongs to no one else, Andrew. You take it—it's addressed to you. It's been waiting for you, all this time."

"Here, let *me* see that." And all at once Ginger Hair let down his heel that had been pressed against the paneling, dropped his crossed arms and stepped forward with his hand out, palm down, in a neat, peremptory gesture, as if, I thought, with a second sharp spasm of resentment, there was no question at all but that it was his business and right to see it.

"No," I said, and lifted my jacket and slid the letter into an inside breast pocket. "Nobody needs to see it but me. I think I'll take it as mine."

Ginger's hand dropped and his amusement vanished, leaving his little bluish eyes cold behind their protection of thick glass. With a sudden movement he ran his hand through the pale red hair that looked rather stiff and unmanageable. Plainly, he was offended at being so firmly brushed aside, and by a young one, he must have been thinking, of no more than fifteen or sixteen.

"Phineas, I'm sorry. My manners—!" said Beth. "But I was all intent on the letter. Mr. Cames and Andrew, this is Mr. Phineas Brock, one of our summer guests. He's been coming ever since we opened the place."

There were noddings and murmurings of acknowledgment on the part of Dad and Phineas Brock, and Dad held out his hand, which Brock took after the slightest breath of hesitation, held just long enough to convey his displeasure. I didn't say anything.

"What my wife means," said Jim, "by thinking that the letter was meant for you, Andrew, if we may have our little joke, is that she lost it for two months or so after rescuing it from amongst all the stuff your Great-aunt Millicent left and which we mostly

9

burned up, then happened on it again and put it in the cabinet in the kitchen—"

"But the thing is, Andrew," Beth went on excitedly, "that I forgot about your letter until I found it at the back of one of the drawers, and put it on the kitchen table, meaning to take it upstairs again for safekeeping. Then if it didn't disappear for the third time! Well, now, Mr. Cames, have a look round. It'll all seem so different to you—shabby, I shouldn't wonder, after the way it was when you were a boy and there were housemaids and a butler and a housekeeper and cook and gardeners. Now I'll be getting on with dinner—it's at eight so you have about an hour."

She turned away. Jim slung Dad's golf bag over his shoulder and picked up his suitcase. But Dad didn't follow at once. He went over to the broad arch just to glance in at the drawing room where enormous windows looked out across the loch. Standing not far away, I heard him murmur under his breath, "My God!" and then after a moment or two, another "My God!"

I followed, and saw an indiscriminate array of furniture that gave no more the impression of a castle interior than what was in the hall, so that again I was shocked. And yet, somehow, as I stood there, I got a feeling of casual comfort, of invitation, exactly because it was not formal and elegant. But what my father saw with appalled and remembering eyes was a rather dingy black-and-white speckled carpet that covered the entire floor, and heavy chairs and a couple of lounges clothed in wrinkled, ill-fitting figured slipcovers in bright colors. On the built-in seats under

10

the windows on two sides of the room, big black-and-white pillows slumped at intervals and at the ends, where carved pilasters divided the windows.

Now Dad stepped right in and, going after him, I noticed an electric heater sitting in the fireplace on the inner side of the room. "An Adam," Dad said bitterly. He is an architect, and even I, knowing nothing about Adam fireplaces, could see that this one was handsome and spacious and that because the heater was very small and cheapish looking, nothing could have been more incongruous. He gave a last despairing glance around, then turned and went back into the hall.

Phineas Brock, still standing there with his hands in his jacket pockets, had obviously been taking in the whole thing. He smiled as though pleased that Dad was shaken at what the McBrides, in their poverty-stricken state, had been forced to do—fill that demanding room with furnishings that were an insult to what it once had been and still is.

Now Phineas actually chuckled, turned on his heel, went on ahead of us along the hall, swung around, the palm of his hand swiveling on the fumed oak newel-post, and started up the stairs. "This way—" he sang out, as if the place were as much his as Jim's.

CHAPTER

2

"Andy!" But where—who could it be? Someone frightened, desperately frightened. *"Andy—Andy!"* Why, the voice was inside me, and I stopped abruptly as if it had clutched at me, and dropped my bags so suddenly that Dad, coming up behind, exclaimed in annoyance.

"Well, go on—go on, then, Andrew. Jim'll be waiting. What's the matter? Don't you know a dumbwaiter when you see one? Don't you remember my telling you I used to play in it when I was a kid—we all did, all the cousins."

It hung there to the right of the stairs in a well that had once risen from a basement kitchen on up from floor to floor. I stared at it for a second or two, swept by unexplainable emotions, not knowing what to do, what it was I *must* do in answer to such terror. That voice—a child's! A girl's voice, shaking, beside itself, calling the name I used to be called by the neighborhood children and still was by Dad and some of my friends.

I looked up, and there was Phineas waiting for us, watching me as I stood on the stairs; then he turned and went off, and I kept going. Jim was farther along the hall, having already, apparently, put Dad's clubs and suitcase where they belonged.

"Mr. Brock'd like you to see his arrangements," said Jim, slightly emphasizing the word "arrangements" as though to make Phineas seem privileged and special.

Phineas gave a little bow and waved Dad and me into a large, many-windowed room, a corner room with a superb view in two directions across to thickly wooded slopes where I caught glimpses of tiny, isolated chimneys. Smoke wafted, curled slowly, and hung in drifts in the damp air. The hills mounted behind the castle, losing their woods and becoming smooth green swells that beckoned to me as though, like Dad, I'd known them as a child. I saw the black cattle moving and stopping, moving and stopping, but from here, at least, could not see any stone cottage with a wall built right up to the window. No, but I'd find it. *It would be there.*

What I meant was this: after dinner on the plane, when the picture was about to be shown and all the shades had been pulled down, instead of looking at the screen I'd leaned my head back and closed my eyes, and presently a scene had come to me, a sudden scene of a girl kneeling on a green hillside helping an old man to mend a stone wall. But it wasn't merely a stone wall—it was a dry stone wall (a dry stane dyke the Scots would say). And there's a difference, I told myself afterwards, though how I knew this I hadn't a notion. I'd never talked to anyone in my life about that kind of wall, nor ever read about it, as far as I could remember, nor even known there was such a thing. But a dry stone wall is one put up without mortar; the knowledge was there in my mind, and it hadn't been before.

I got the scene of the girl and the old man with great intensity, every detail; knew what they were saying, though not through the medium of words, and understood with perfect clarity that there is an art to building these walls that's dying out. And I knew this too, that what I was seeing was taking place in Scotland.

It was not a dream. I couldn't have been asleep (though my eyes were closed) because I was vaguely aware of a baby whimpering and of Dad fiddling with the dial in the seat arm while I was seeing, in place of the seat back in front of me, those two on the hillside and noticing that there was a stone cottage close by and that the wall was built right up to it, ending just below one of the windows. On the other side there were sheep, but on this side cattle—black cattle. The wall had got a weak place in it with the rocks falling away and would have to be mended or the cattle would go through one way and the sheep the other. How long I was lost in this visitation I couldn't be certain, but at some point, when I realized that Dad had taken out his earphones, I leaned over and asked, "Dad, what are black cattle called in Scotland?"

"Black Angus. Actually, they're Aberdeen Angus. Why?"

"Just wondered."

I sank back and closed my eyes again but because I'd spoken, the scene simply wasn't there. I went on

14

staring at the seat in front of me, then closed my eyes, but nothing was returned to me, no green hillside—green as green fire—with its dark wall snaking up over the rise, then continuing at a slightly different angle on the hill beyond.

I thought about this and then fell asleep, and when I woke was struck at once by the fact that I'd had an absolutely extraordinary experience and that I'd been a fool to lean over and talk to Dad, asking that question about the cattle. A most poignant sense of loss washed over me. The man had called the girl—what *had* he called her? A nickname, not a regular name. I'd known it while I was asking Dad about the cattle, but now it was gone. I was astounded. She'd had on a soft wool tam that sat on her head, on her reddish gold hair, like a tilted waffle, I'd noticed especially. But I'd forgotten her name, and it was as if I'd forgotten the name of a friend.

I was forced back to the present, hearing Brock's insidious voice talking golf and handicaps because he wanted Dad to have a game with him the next day; he'd get a couple of others, he said, to make up a foursome. But what about the rain that had begun gusting hard against these vast panes? Then I turned and saw the hooded bath on the other side of the room: dark and gleaming, with reddish wood encasing the zinc-lined tub and the whole looking, as Dad remembered, as if it weighed a ton. It stood out from the other imposing furniture—the Victorian bed, the enormous blackish wardrobe and the chests of drawers—very distinguished, much handsomer in its peculiar way than either the wardrobe or the chests, and as ridiculous as Dundrearies.

I burst out laughing. "Oh, so *you're* the"—and

caught myself on the brink of disaster, my mind struggling to save me—"*you're* the man with the hooded tub. You're the lucky one!"

Phineas smiled at the floor, then slid me a small, considering stare from under his bristly brows. "So Jim told you. Yes, it diverts me. You have no idea what comical evocations it's capable of—or you might say, what comical adventures it evokes. It's a quirk of mine."

So Phineas was the Quark, and the Quark had quirks. No doubt any number: for instance, being childishly pleased that he had something on Dad, his pleasure no doubt a revenge for my rudeness about the letter.

More talk about golf tomorrow and where they'd play; then Phineas nodded us off. And when Jim had taken us along the hall, around a corner, through a door which he closed behind him, and into a short darkish passage with a bathroom on one side and a bedroom on the other, he laughed quietly and gave me a quick, glancing punch on the shoulder.

"You almost had me in the soup. You almost finished me." And I noticed that even though he'd closed the door behind us, he kept his voice down.

"I could see it coming," Dad said. " 'Oh, so *you're* the Quark! *You're* the one Jim meant!' " We went into the bedroom and I put my bags down by the bed I wanted, the one on the left. Both had tall, curly brass frames, dented, with crooked knobs, but polished.

"I know. I only just managed to save us, but I had the damndest feeling he wasn't fooled. Is he ever?"

"Of course he is," said Jim. "He doesn't know anybody calls him the Quark, which it was very wrong

16

of me to tell you—his nickname, as if I were making fun of him. It slipped out. I've never done that before to the clientele, but I suppose it's because you're like family after all the writing back and forth and this being your place, in a manner of speaking. Maybe he does know. But in that case why would he go on being so confoundedly pleased about everything?

"Y'see, it was the men up at the Research Installation who come here to eat and stay and talk in the evenings. They talk science, the whole range of it, and they were the ones who got to calling Phineas the Quark. And then you can't help but see how it fits him—he just *is* the Quark: a busy little particle of matter." Jim looked up and around. "I hope you'll be comfortable. There're two more blankets in there—" And he waved a hand at the wardrobe that stood slightly aslant with one door hanging open—a far cry from Phineas's fine big one, and I bet anything ours wouldn't close and stay closed, and as it turned out, it never would. "This room's the best we've finished off so far after the Qua—— well, there we go! I'd better watch it. And you have a nice large bathroom with two showers. Think o' that! If they don't work just right, let me know. Sometimes they get a bit tricky."

He nodded cheerily with an encouraging lift of the brows, and went out; and when the door closed behind him, Dad dropped onto the other bed and when his big body hit the mattress, the springs cried in agony. He closed his eyes. "We'll be awake the whole damned night. Couldn't be worse. Nothing like what I'd expected, but then nothing is after a quarter of a century, though I'd never have imagined the come-

17

down. Thank God your mother isn't here." I was drawn to the windows, this time to get a different view from the Quark's. The rain had lessened to blown drops, and there was a light in the sky behind the clouds. "What I want now," Dad said, "is an absolutely magnificent dinner."

He got up and went across the hall with fresh underwear and a clean shirt, and when he'd gone I slid a hand inside my jacket and drew out the letter. I examined my own name written, as I thought, around a hundred years ago, with disbelief. Yet it wouldn't seem in the least strange to a Britisher to find himself written to after so long a time when over here triple-barreled names are handed down intact generation after generation. "Portrero Lodge, Castle Lane, Dunhoweth," it said on the flap on the back. We were in Dunhoweth. And where was Castle Lane? Close by, no doubt, but if close by, why write? And then not send?

"Andy! Andy!" That anguished cry, but not now inside me, coming so clearly I'd stopped as if I'd been struck, and dropped my bags on the stairs. No, only the memory of a cry, a child's voice, a small girl's. And remembered Dad telling me how he and the cousins had had a game of climbing into the dumbwaiter, one by one, and being hauled up and down all huddled in the close dark when the grown-ups were thoroughly occupied elsewhere with their eternal gossip and card playing.

I'd save my letter for tomorrow, I thought, for when I was in the hills alone.

CHAPTER

3

Jim, now maître d', done up in a dark suit and looking almost handsome, was about to lead us across the dining hall to a table where we had a view out over the hills in the last light. But Dad, about to enter, stood still for a moment. "This place," he said, almost reverently. "Yes, this place. This beautiful room. Though of course Aunt Mill used to have a tremendous table right down the center."

"I know," Jim said. "But we thought there was no point in our buying it, because we'd never get parties like that, only small ones. Now I think we made a mistake. But this is what the diners come for—this room. This is our bread and butter. It's what'll save us, if we're to be saved at all, this and Beth's cooking. It's a room you can't ruin. If you simply keep it clean and polished, with the candles lighted and the fire going and the linen spotless, it holds its own."

At the end where we entered, there was a musicians' gallery above our heads; and I saw, as I followed Jim over to our table and looked back, that the walls of it were painted with trees and figures in rich, soft colors that in the beginning must have been rich and bright. As I found later, there were three large, many-branched candelabra up there, hidden by a balustrade and, in the light of the candles, the figures and leaves and flowers seemed to move.

At the other end of the room, directly opposite the gallery, there was an enormous fireplace, broad and tall—broad enough to take a Yule log—and with a great copper hood that had been polished until it gleamed. The walls were paneled in some lustrous wood that had nothing at all to do with either the blackish painted paneling of the main hall or the fumed oak of the newel-post and the banister and stairs and dumbwaiter. High overhead the ceiling retreated away and away into darkness because now an early evening—early because of the storm—was coming on, and the little wavering blooms of candles on the tables only served to make the shadowed height seem more vast.

"How d'you like this, young man?" Jim was pulling out Dad's chair at a table near the fireplace, where there was a whopping fire going, and he smiled expectantly at me. Dad would look out over the hills as long as the light lasted, and from where I sat I could take in both the view in front of me and, on my right, the fire leaping from two logs as thick through as a man's body.

"Now," I said solemnly, "*now* I feel as if I'm really in a castle."

The soup was delectable, and the rest of the dinner as well, with so many courses that it was more than even I could handle at one meal. But Jim had no sooner wheeled over the dessert cart than I heard the Quark's voice behind me. Damn him to hell, and I refused to lift my head. Go away—go away. But Phineas did not go away. He had a friend, someone he wanted to introduce to Dad because they'd be playing golf together the next day and, having finished their meal, took it upon themselves to come over and sit down.

I glared at them; the Quark had put himself right in the middle of my view, sunk in deep dusk by now with the dark shapes of the hills massed against the powerful blue green sky. Down low there was a scattering of lights. As I ate, I kept turning to the fire and almost at once stopped listening to what they were saying. Golf to me, then, was an excruciating bore.

I heard the Quark's friend, whose name I hadn't bothered to get, mention dry stone walls, and without thinking I looked up and said, "The art's dying out, the art of building them the way they used to be built."

"So it has," the Quark's friend said. "But how did you know that?"

"*He's* been reading," said the Quark. "I'll make a bet he's what's called a great reader." I thought there was a touch of malice in his voice.

"At intervals," my father said.

But I didn't care what anybody said. I was suddenly absorbed in that experience I'd had on the plane, apparently staring, all the time I was talking, at a vest button on the Quark's chest. "A bottom stone," I began, and remembered afterwards it was as if I were alone, "a bottom stone has to be laid so that it holds the stones on each side and they hold it. A

21

skilled worker"—and I was hearing the old man's voice very clearly in my mind—"a skilled dyker, I mean, lays his stones out first on both sides of the direction the wall will take and marks this path with stakes and twine. The stones have to be rough so they'll fit in firmly." I stopped, taking my time to get it right. Nobody said anything, and I went on, "You dig the trench and build up the outside stones, then fill in with heart stones, the little ones you have to stamp down hard. You build up to a height of two feet, then put on the through band, build up again, put on the cover stone, flat like the through band, and finish off with the coping stones. And because they're likely to get loosened, you have to choose them and lay them very carefully so that they lock into each other, and if you're building on a steep slope you have to work uphill so that everything gets locked against the work already done."

Had the old man actually said all that? No, he hadn't. Mostly it had been a matter of gestures and acts, the girl's brief questions as she offered her stones, and the old man's brief explanations as he accepted or rejected.

When I looked up, first at the Quark and his friend, then at Dad, I saw that they seemed at a complete loss for words. Their expressions were comical mixtures of bafflement and surprise. "That'll be a buck each," I said dryly. "I don't tell just anybody how to do this."

After a second or two, "You said dyker," observed the Quark. "Why didn't you say stonemason? I believe that's the American expression."

"Because, I guess, you *say* dyker in Scotland." That's the word that had been in my mind. Dyker. No other.

22

"What do you mean, you *guess?*" demanded Phineas, like a schoolteacher with a little kid. "You used the work 'dyker' as if you knew without doubt. And you've never been in Scotland or any part of the British Isles?"

I wasn't submitting to any third degree. "No, never," said Dad, "and I don't happen to know that word."

"You were remembering," said the Quark, leaning forward. "You were remembering so clearly that you were actually seeing. You were looking at my chest as if the entire process was being acted out in front of you—right here," and he laid his hand across the top of his vest.

For the first time I looked him in the eye. "Is that so?"

"Oh, yes—yes, you were." He said it with absolute assurance. "Have you ever heard of eidetic imagery? Eidetic seeing?"

"No, I haven't." My voice was cool and indifferent.

"Well, a child—it's almost always a child—will look at a thing, and then later—it can be immediately afterwards or days or years later—will be able to reproduce or tell what he has seen in the most intimate detail as if he's looking at an afterimage of it, which is what he's doing, actually, because the afterimage is imposed on the child's mind with photographic fidelity. Is that what happened in your case?"

"I don't know. I can't remember."

"Have you ever had these eidetic experiences before?"

I wasn't going to answer, and Dad said, "Not that I know of. Have you, Andrew? You've never told me—I've never had any idea that such a thing was going on."

I felt they were closing in and I couldn't take it. Again I shrugged. "D'you mind if I leave you to your golf? I think I'll move along." I got up, nodded to the other two, and walked across the dining hall among the tables. God, what a fool! At the moment I'd finished that little lecture on wall building, and come to—as if I'd been in a trance—and seen the astonished expressions of the three men, I'd had a small, warm feeling of triumph, like a magician who has perfectly worked his trick. But just then, when the Quark insisted that I'd not only been remembering but seeing, I'd begun feeling uneasy, almost anxious, and still did when I stopped to tell Jim, coming into the hall from the kitchen, that it was one of the best meals I'd ever had in my life, and would he please tell Mrs. McBride that. And could I have a sandwich or two to take on a hike tomorrow?

I'd fallen asleep over a detective novel by the time Dad finally came up. He sat down on his own bed and studied me. "We talked about you," he said.

I groaned. "Why can't you just leave me alone—I mean, forget about me—"

"But you'll have to admit that what you did isn't just an ordinary occurrence for an American boy on his first trip to Scotland. And Phineas thinks you were anything but showing off or trying to impress. He said he thought you were absolutely engrossed in what you were remembering, and I had to agree. I really had to admit you weren't showing off. As a matter of fact, I told them you weren't in the habit of it— that you're just the opposite."

I was silent for a moment. "Oh, you did. Well, look, Dad—would you do me a favor? Would you just not talk about me? Would you just please never talk about me to anyone, and especially to the Quark? I will not be raked over by that guy. He's a snarky know-it-all, and he was pleased as the devil he heard you swearing over the looks of the drawing room, or whatever you call it. He *has* something on you. I think he likes having things on people. I think he collects them—things he finds out."

"Rubbish, Andrew—rubbish! It's just that he's interested in you, and he explained all about eidetic seeing. What intrigues him about you is that you seemed to be watching a process you wouldn't ordinarily know anything about. He admitted that he himself knows nothing about dyking, and he was born here and has lived here all his life. But of course if you were seeing a printed page, you could have been reading it. Were you?"

"I don't know what you're talking about!" I exclaimed in exasperation, which was of course a lie, but what could I have done but lie?

"Phineas wanted to know if you're brilliant, a top student."

"That's a laugh."

"Well, I didn't say, actually, how poorly you've been doing since you got back into circulation again, but that you were first-rate before—not brilliant, perhaps, but—"

"That I'm brilliant as a clod. That I'm a rotten student—"

"Oh, no, you're not, Andrew, and never have been. Only since Hoagy—"

"Well, just don't say anything, ever, to anyone,

about anything to do with me. I'd appreciate." And I turned out my 25-watt bulb and turned over, showing I wanted to be left to go to sleep, and pretty soon Dad, after he'd undressed and leafed a bit more through his *Architectural Digest,* turned out *his* 25-watt bulb and rolled over and was snoring in about ten seconds or so.

I folded my arms behind my head and looked up into the darkness. Never again—promise me, I instructed myself—never again, on pain of death, say anything in front of the Quark or in front of anybody, of the tiniest, slightest consequence beyond the most trivial and mundane. "Beyond the most trivial and mundane." I can put it that way now, but couldn't have then. But it was what I meant.

On the way upstairs after leaving the dining hall, I'd stopped on arriving at the dumbwaiter, my heart thumping with expectation, hoping that perhaps I'd hear again so clearly and strangely, *"Andy! Andy!"*— that agonized appeal. Yet what could I have done in response? I stood there on the stairs waiting, almost praying it would come, and had no idea why I wanted it so, when the truth was I was afraid, as I suppose anyone is afraid, just at first, of an experience that is outside reason. But nothing happened. I felt the deadness, the lack, the emptiness.

Would it be a matter of patience before the voice would be heard again? Or had I only imagined it? No, something had happened, something as impossible of explanation, as far outside the usual run of my life as that visitation on the plane.

CHAPTER

4

The coming of the Hoagy nightmare, which I'd had five times since his death, never seemed to tie up with the previous day's happenings or with anything I'd been involved with in my thoughts, at least with anything on the surface. This time, on going to sleep, I was apparently wholly taken up with that trancelike revealing of something that should have remained private, an event quite apart from anything to do with Hoagy. And yet, that night—

Hoagy and I are making our way down a steep wash somewhere on an unknown coast, and even as we pick our way, I know what the end will be, though why we're struggling with such desperate haste down to the beach, I haven't any idea. The incline is very dangerous. Stones constantly slide from under our feet, threatening to send us hurtling over the brutal boulders for hundreds of feet to the bottom, and we continually knock our ankles and shins as we descend.

It's a narrow beach and when we reach it, we run as if we're trying to escape from some wild animal, or a gang, and my heart is thudding in such terror I can hardly breathe. Now I notice the waves moving in, each more towering than the last: gray, monstrous waves in the gray dimness, neither dark nor light. Hoagy and I race back to the cliff, searching for some way to escape what we know is coming. But there is no path upward, and the beach is closed at each end, and the cliff too steep to climb. The only way of escape is the wash we had come down, but it is cut off now by the rising tide.

The sea is at our feet and we turn and plunge in and swim to keep from being overwhelmed. My struggles in the gray water seem endless. In my dream I am convinced I am not a swimmer, and labor hopelessly. I hear Hoagy calling, but can do nothing to help. Again, in a different way, there is now no time, only a kind of eternity of exhaustion, the agonized choking for breath, going down and wondering if I have already drowned.

But when the water recedes, I find myself on the beach, searching for Hoagy and calling to him in the gray nothingness, in the light that is not a light. And when I come to someone lying on the sand that cannot be Hoagy, I turn the body over—and, oh, it *is* Hoagy, it is!—and yet, somehow a stranger, terribly a stranger, as if drowning has changed him in some profound and indescribable way. I sob over him, try to breathe air into his lungs, but as I draw back to recover my own breath, the dead lips speak, using the name he and my mother had called me by since I was a child. "You've won, Durry, but you've lost." And what can those ominous words mean, and why should a dead man speak? In what way have I won? *Won what?*

That was my dream, my invariable nightmare. And I would wake, just as I'd awakened now, shaking with despair and fright and horror, my throat burning with dry, buried sobs, at that point in my dream when I would say to myself that this was Hoagy and he'd gone down and was now dead. But as always, even as I had picked my way between the boulders in the wash, I'd known what the end would be: Hoagy's drowning.

At other times, in other nightmares, the two of us would be lying on the beach in the warm sun on a perfect day, and presently the waves would begin to tower, the light would darken, and there would be no way of escape: up the steep stairs at the back of the beach between ugly, mountainous, mustard yellow buildings, their blind side to the sea, that we couldn't reach. Or we'd be swimming happily in the surf and the tide would turn wicked, becoming remorselessly heavier and more powerful, working to drag us under, and then at the end there would be Hoagy, always lying facedown on the rocks or the sand, and I would have to go to that sprawled figure and turn it over.

I sat up and knew at once that I mustn't rouse Dad. Perhaps my horror had lessened over the past months, because now I was able to think and to act with some balance, as I hadn't before.

I got out of bed, trying to ease my way quietly over those confounded springs, my one thought being not to give away the fact that I'd had the nightmare again, something Dad would guess instantly if he heard the way I was breathing, in involuntary shudders that came at the end of each muscle spasm, and my teeth chattering as if I had a fever. He must not know in case, off his guard, on some golf tee, talking with the Quark while the foursome was waiting for the players ahead to move out of range, he might give everything away.

I crossed the dark little hall to the bathroom and splashed cold water against my face again and again to shock myself out of the aftermath of the dream, relieved myself, and sat on the toilet lid until the chattering and shuddering began to ease; sat there with my feet freezing on the icy linoleum and looked up out the window of the little room that housed the toilet and saw moonlight gleaming on the slates of the steeply pitched roof.

It would be a fine morning, and I'd have to go into the hills whether I felt like it or not, because if I didn't, having asked for lunch and said I was going, there'd be questions. I must do something; I couldn't just hang around. Yet sitting there in the cold, I felt the old familiar dreariness and knew that I was drained of all desire to do anything whatever.

What I couldn't understand was why the dreams were always so different from reality, though telling in their own way that I'd lost Hoagy; unvarying in their insistence on the gradually overwhelming tide, on the fact that I, a poor swimmer, had been unable to save Hoagy, who was a superb one but who, nevertheless, had been the one to go down.

What I could remember of the actual end was this: It was late at night on the mountain outside the lodge where there had been a party, and we were packing up Tory's things to go home. Tory, Hoagy's girl, had brought food and come early in her own car to help get everything ready, and I was in her car at Hoagy's insistence, and Hoagy was fumbling around trying to get his own started. For some reason I've never been able to explain to myself, I was so depressed I could scarcely answer Tory when she tried to comfort me before starting off down the mountain—down that winding, narrow, treacherous road—telling me that after all Hoagy couldn't be angry. Hadn't he, as I'd reported to her, ended up laughing and saying, "OK, old man. You've always been a wise old man and you always will be a wise old man. But I don't want you going down with me—nope, nope, you go and get in Tory's car."

But what had he meant? What had his *tone* meant? That clipped, dismissing, ironical tone?

So Tory started off, going slowly and carefully, and then there was the gunning of a motor behind us, and I knew instantly what would happen. I cried out even as Hoagy raced past us on the too narrow road, and Tory got over as close as she could to the steep cliff on our right. Hoagy roared on down ahead, into the blackness around a blind curve. We heard the crash, and Tory stopped the car so violently that I was thrown forward against the dashboard. There was a deep silence.

Then Tory was crying, "Oh, God—oh, God—" and I was dumb with a certain knowledge while we both struggled with weak, scrabbling fingers to get out, then tried to stand on legs that would scarcely hold us. We ran around the bend and there was the bridge with the whole right side of it torn out where Hoagy's car had dived through, and from below, from the bed of the river, the long gleam of a single headlight pierced up from where the car lay smashed. There was no sound, though I thought later, days later when I could think again, when I could remember, that there must at least have been the sound of water running between the stones of the riverbed. It had been a winter of little rain; otherwise the river would have been full and the end of the accident a different one.

We scrambled down the bank, pebbles and shale slipping beneath our feet. Ahead I saw Hoagy, the blur of his white shirt and light slacks where he was flung in a grotesque, an impossible position over a boulder. Beyond him lay the car, nose up, so that it had spun end over end, and the one cone of light pointed up like something palpable in the darkness. Tory and I worked our way over to Hoagy, shaking, stumbling, slipping in the water, on the wet stones, between boulders, cruelly knocking ankles, knees, shins, but feeling nothing and only discovering afterwards, by our deep bruises, what we had done. And when we reached Hoagy at last and leaned over and looked into the still face and open eyes, we knew that he was gone and that there was nothing in the world to be done.

Had Hoagy known what would happen? As he turned me away, had he planned what he would do? Was it already there in his mind? And when I asked Tory afterwards if she knew why Hoagy wanted to go down alone, she had no idea. She was carrying things out, going back and forth. She didn't know, hadn't questioned. Hoagy was quiet as he so often was because of pain. She'd simply taken it for granted that perhaps he wasn't going home. And then, I would say to myself over and over, Hoagy was killed with something between us that I couldn't get straight, so that after the closeness and understanding, after my love and admiration for him, it was more than I could bear to think of on waking from these nightmares, or at any time when I allowed myself to remember.

CHAPTER

5

On this cold, brilliant morning, the showers dripped and dribbled and plopped, and there was Dad wrenching away at the faucets and swearing. But we should have suspected Jim's "If they don't work just right, let me know. Sometimes they get a bit tricky." Dad was in the thick of his temper. And the bathroom was like a vault and dim and ugly, with a single naked lightbulb overhead and worn lino on the floor. There was a bidet, the only thing even vaguely newish looking, but I couldn't have cared less about a bidet. I'd never used one and had no idea what its particular advantage was.

"You'll just have to go and get Jim," Dad shouted, and I was exasperated.

"But I'd have to get dressed," I shouted back.

"Well, then, goddam it, *get* dressed—" when the pipes gave a resounding rattle and clank, and here came a gush of apparently icy water, and Dad howled and backed up, stumbled over the lip of the shower entrance, and staggered and caught himself. And even as he managed the recovery, all in one fluid movement like an athlete's, I was thinking what a body he had for an old guy of over forty: flat belly, good big shoulders and chest, long, well-muscled thighs and calves, when so many of the fathers his age were already slope-shouldered and beginning to get pots and bald heads. Even Hoagy, when he left for overseas at nineteen, hadn't been built like Dad, not yet, but he would have been, given a future. When he got back from Vietnam, thin and wounded, he was still only twenty. As for me, I realized there were two physical camps in our family: my mother and I, lean and rangy (to put the best names to it; but I saw myself as stringy at the age of fifteen), and Dad and Hoagy, those two having been formed as I hoped passionately one day to be.

At this point I thought of Dad's determination not to dwell on his lost son—Hoagy had been gone almost eight months and he'd gotten past the worst of it—and to put aside the fact of a wife who had deliberately and, I had a feeling, with enormous relief, decided to stay at home.

"But, Nell, your book's finished," he'd said.

"Yes, and I've begun something new—about three months ago. So don't insist. Just please, Alec, don't go on insisting."

He wouldn't believe it at first. We'd always planned to come to Scotland together, to stay at Cames, the four of us. And despite her change toward him because of Hoagy's death, it must somehow never have occurred to him that in the end she'd say, "Alec, I can't. I'm not going." Perhaps he'd been thinking that this journey, our coming over together even without Hoagy, would change everything and bring her back to him after the blame she'd put on him for all that followed Hoagy's final decision to go overseas.

I watched Dad waiting for the water to turn lukewarm, which he said it was beginning to, and we had our showers and a good rubdown. And after breakfast he went off with the Quark and his friend to play golf, and I started out with the lunch Beth had put up for me.

Cames property was all wild now, except for a broad mown strip on either side of the drive, with flowers in a bed up near the castle entrance. But the whole effect was one of wildness, with no gardeners any longer to keep back the almost junglelike growth. On my way to a flight of steps at the back of Cames that Jim had said would lead to Castle Lane, I passed an ancient greenhouse, long out of use, with broken windows, and after that, going down, left the sunlight and submerged into a dense green shade like a swimmer sinking under water.

At the bottom of the steps I turned off to the right up toward the hills, and presently I came to a stone house with its windows broken and holes in the roof. I went up onto the porch and peered in; the door had long since dropped or been wrenched away, and I saw the stained and hanging wallpaper, the rain-discolored floors. Could this possibly be Portrero Lodge? I refused to believe it and came down the steps and went on up the lane.

When at last I got out of Cames Woods and into the open sunlight with the wind in my face and the sound of birdsong in my ears—larks, lapwings, peewits, I wouldn't have known then what they were—and the green rises swelling ahead of me, rise after rise, with not a soul in sight but the black Angus feeding far off on the other side of the field that was enclosed on both sides by the dry stone walls, I felt a kind of peacefulness descend. The grayness of spirit left from my nightmare was washing away. I felt—and I couldn't believe it—almost happy in a way I hadn't been since before Hoagy was killed. Or at least, if not actually happy, I felt the imminence of happiness, a kind of hope for it, as if the knots inside me could become untangled and the grief and confusion I'd been lost in could be allowed to fall away and, if not forgotten, at least be left behind.

There was a gate, and then a footpath led up beside one of the walls that wandered away over the hills. At a place where it had begun to fall to pieces, I dropped to one knee to examine the interior to see if my knowledge, so strangely learned, could possibly be correct. And I saw the heart stones lying neatly fitted down in between the larger, outer ones, set at right angles to the length of the wall, to the path it took, and on the side, on the ground where they'd fallen, the big cover bands and coping stones. And I thought how one of these days I would like to try to put that wall together again.

I climbed, mindless for a while, and then because of the hills and because it was in the Berkeley hills I'd last seen Sheila, I was back there when I was in love with her in the eighth grade—wildly, sadly, joyously in love with Sheila, so that I could think only of

Sheila, write letters to Sheila that were never sent, watch her come into class, watch her write her tests, wave her hand to answer whatever might have been asked, watch her do whatever she might do, and leave—and I'd catch up with her. I was in a state of shock in those days, when I first kissed her, off behind the trees in the rustling, laughter-filled dusk at a class picnic, and knew for the first time to the core of my being what maleness meant. For a second at most I was embarrassed at what my desire for her was doing to me. Was she aware? But how could she help but be? Then I no longer cared and was conscious only of our two bodies—close, close.

Hoagy and Dad teased me about her, but I didn't care. I was too crazy-melancholy-happy to care about anything like that, people noticing, people being amused. I loved Sheila and Sheila loved me.

And next, without warning, her father decided they must move to Oakland, and Sheila was gone, snatched away, and was living there instead of in Berkeley. We phoned, tried to see each other weekends, but her whole life was changed, and then she changed somehow with a circle of new friends, and I couldn't hold her, couldn't keep her, couldn't keep our love the way it had been. We were too young; the move blighted us because we had no control over our lives.

> On the banks of the Shannon
> When Sheila was nigh,
> No blithe Irish lad was so happy as I—

Dad sang one day, not knowing what had happened, and Hoagy said in a low, gruff voice, "Lay off, Pop," and I had to leave the room and go upstairs and cry as I hadn't cried in years. It took me months to get over Sheila, to be able even to think of that song without knowing a kind of death inside all over again. "No blithe Irish lad was so happy as I—"

I'd never loved anyone like that since. And sometime later, about three weeks before Hoagy was killed, I hiked up into the hills one day with some of the fellows I practiced bouldering with, and coming down, passed a bunch of kids going up toward Grizzly Peak—and there in the group was Sheila. I stood dumbstruck, and she raised her hand and exclaimed happily in surprise, "Oh, Durry—hi!" calling me by the name Hoagy and my mother had always used, and I couldn't even speak but stood there gazing after her. She'd kept turning to look back, and the last time waved once more and blew me a kiss of farewell, then disappeared with the others into a grove of trees and I never saw her again.

I climbed the Scottish hills thinking of Sheila, and how Hoagy had said just those three words, "Lay off, Pop—" He'd understood. He'd understood everything. Hoagy and Sheila—I'd never loved anyone as I'd loved those two, with a queer, aching, vulnerable kind of love.

After an hour or so I came to Howeth Glen, which is nothing but a short High Street and a few cottages scattered around in the trees and of course a church. I went on through and up higher over the mounting hills until I came to the top and stood looking out across miles and miles of tumbled green land clear to the far-off sea.

Why, it was the Western Sea! There it lay, glinting in the sun, all that way away.

Prickles went up and down my arms and around the back of my neck because my mother had read to me, when I was little, out of a small gray book she'd had when she was a child, of how Mordred and King Arthur fought by the shores of the Western Sea, and King Arthur grasped his spear in both hands and smote Mordred, and the spear pierced through Mordred's body, "cleaving his armour as if it were thin air." And Mordred raised his sword and brought it down on Arthur's head, and the sword struck through the King's helmet and bit into his skull, and Mordred fell dead and Arthur sank senseless to the ground.

"But he didn't *die,* did he? He didn't *die!*"

"Yes, Durry, he did die, in the end, but not right away. At least the story leaves us not sure. He passed out of the human realm."

Then he was just the same as dead, I thought bitterly, and couldn't bear that that good man should have been killed by one of his own circle.

I sat down with my back to the wall, not caring whose wall it was or whether some farmer would come and ask me what I was doing on private property. And no one came—I was utterly alone with the sun and the wind and the birds and that far view of the Western Sea, which is now called the Atlantic. My stomach told me I was hungry, so that it must have been near noon, and when I looked at my watch it was ten after one.

But hunger or no hunger, I had something to do first. I reached into my jacket pocket and drew out the letter, and with my penknife neatly lifted up the flap from where it had gotten stuck, feeling somehow that I had no right to read what hadn't been meant for me. "Don't be a fool," I said, and with the oddest feeling opened out the six pages that had been folded together seventy years before, I saw by the date, and perhaps never touched since.

CHAPTER

6

*"Portrero Lodge
15 April 1900
The evening of the day
you were here*

"Andrew, my dear,

"Even though you're to be at home three more days before leaving with your regiment, we won't be seeing one another, and I want to say good-bye now in a way that will express more clearly what I feel about us than could possibly have been expressed in that stormy set-to we had this afternoon full of reproaches and recriminations and misunderstandings.

"I can be honest now and say that ever since we were children playing together—you and Barty and I, whenever you two were home from school—I had an awareness underneath that no matter how rascally you could be, no matter how your moods changed, you took it for granted I belonged to you. I've somehow had the feeling that you were always making an unconscious assumption about the rest of our lives, so that I've often wondered if someday you would take it for granted we would marry, which meant that as an adult you would pay no more attention to your mother's resentment and disapproval of me than you ever had.

"You would always do exactly as you pleased, having no father to give advice and perhaps command your respect. And because it never occurred to you that I might have plans or insights or desires that could possibly differ from yours when it came to our final relationship, I can understand why you were so incredulous when I told you this afternoon that I would not marry you.

"Your accusations concerning Barty's and my plans to marry are groundless. He and I have never said a word about marriage, and of course your mother would be almost as appalled at the idea of Barty bringing an estate agent's daughter into the Cames family as at the idea of her own son doing it, though I imagine Barty's being only a nephew might dilute the disaster a little. All the same, it would seem quite incredible to her that your grandmother could tolerate such an idea, let alone contemplate it with pleasure.

"I remember your mother, back from one of her usual long stays in Edinburgh, saying to your grandmother, 'Estate agent! No one but you could possibly think of giving the head gardener the title of estate agent!'

"But John Montmorency is not an ordinary head

gardener, your grandmother pointed out, if head gardeners by their very nature could ever be said to be ordinary. And you had only to look at the Cames gardens, she said, to know the kind of man who had had the vision and the knowledge to plan them, together with the ability to carry out his plans, and who saw to it that the gardens were kept in the most beautiful order, season after season.

"I wonder if you have ever really been aware, Andrew, of the special feeling I've had for your grandmother all these years, ever since I first got up the courage at the age of five to come looking for you. She found me wandering in the Italian garden and we had a conversation. I'll never forget the way she studied me, very quietly and searchingly, as if there were all the time in the world.

" 'And what is your name, child?' she asked, and when I told her, 'Oh, yes, Mr. Montmorency's little girl. What a fascinating combination, Irish and French. You'll be a most interesting person one of these days, I shouldn't doubt. But perhaps, by the look in those eyes, you already are. We must get acquainted. Tell your father I said so and that I've invited you to come and visit me. Would you like to explore the castle? I think there is something up in the musicians' gallery you would especially want to see.'

"When I said in a muffled voice that yes, please, I would like to come, she asked me if I were hunting for my father, and I said that I was hunting for you. 'Oh, someone is always hunting for Andrew,' she said. 'The thing is just to let him appear. He'll come when he's hungry. If you want him, he won't come, and if you don't, he will.'

"Strange how that little conversation, or something very like it, remains with me so clearly out of all the thousands of others from my early years.

"She has always understood me, Andrew, as you never could. Think back over our lives! When have you ever failed to treat me like a yearling that needs discipline, breaking in? I remember how shocked you were when you found me, at the age of twelve or thirteen, reading De Quincey's *Confessions of an English Opium-Eater* and tried to take it away from me and we had a tremendous fight!

"I've loved you, yes, and at one time thought I loved you enough to marry you. That was when I was fifteen. But when I got home from France after the year with Dad's people and my first experience of the lycée, I realized, having had time to think and explore my feelings away from familiar surroundings, that we are hopelessly unsuited, you and I. And I knew that if you ever did ask me to marry you, I would say no, because you would continually try to shape me into your image of the ideal woman and I would continually rebel and end by leaving you.

"What a teasing I've taken in your letters from Sandhurst: a young one like me having my own peculiar ideas about the South African War, ideas that agree with practically no one else's, though I remember the prime minister saying of our annexation of the Transvaal before the Boers won it back, that it was a 'hideous and treacherous crime.' But this was before he so conveniently, for the sake of British interests, changed his mind—and you agree with him now that Britain must inevitably rule all lands adjacent to any British colony. That's jingoism, Andrew, and I hate it.

"You and I will never agree on so many matters.

But I care for you, Andrew, no matter how we differ, and I always shall, perhaps because the relationship has been there since childhood. Do you remember when you shut me in the dumbwaiter out of pure mischief and left me there an endless time (perhaps two or three minutes) and I thought I would go mad because the space was so small, and I was shut in the dark, and I thought you'd gone off and left me. Everything was so quiet—no matter how I called, no one came." The hairs rose along my arms even as I read on, gulping in the words. "Where was everyone! No Barty, no grandmother, no Mrs. McCandless nor Mr. Carmichael, who usually heard everything, no Janice or Nellie or Ellen. Where could they have got to? Or was the dumbwaiter, hanging at the second floor, too far away from the kitchen? Were they all napping? You were a wicked one, Andrew—and then you let me out and kissed me and I struck you, thinking I hated you and kept on thinking it for two whole days. How old were we then—I six and you seven?

"The other night, when a gale was blowing and Dad wasn't feeling well, he asked me to go up to the greenhouse to take in some flats. And in the half dark, that kind of clear, intense blue green dusk that comes during a big wind, I heard someone calling me and I thought it was you. I turned and looked up and saw a branch coming down and darted back just in time. It smashed a corner of the greenhouse. I forgot to tell you this afternoon, but couldn't have, the way things were. It was an odd happening. You were nowhere about, though I felt very strongly that you had been—no doubt because I'd been thinking about you going away. All the same I thought I had seen someone, whether you or not, just in that flick of a second before the branch smashed into the greenhouse. But of course it was a trick of the shadows, when you can never be certain. It was an uncanny experience, and perhaps my life was saved because I thought I heard you call.

"Deirdre"

Deirdre—Deirdre! Why did the name ring on my inner ear with some elusive meaning? It was not the name of the girl I'd seen on the plane; the old man had called her by a nickname which I still couldn't get back. Yet it seemed to me that I ought to remember— ridiculous that I couldn't. I sat there staring out over the hills for a moment, then went on reading, because there was more.

"P.S.

"Oh, Andrew, don't imagine for a moment that you no longer have any interest in anything. You said you would as soon be killed now as not, but this I don't believe, being used to you making outrageous statements in moments of anger and frustration. I've never known anyone more alive in every way, and though I disagree with you about South Africa, I see you filling any office superbly. In fact, I can't bear to think how vigorous and efficient and driving you will be; I pity your opponents. But I want nothing to happen to you. I want you to come back and marry and have children and be happy, though perhaps you will never be happy, being continually dissatisfied.

"I must tell you one other thing. A few days ago the Reverend Claude Woolbert Lowther (what a genius the man's parents had in naming him!) came in his sleek, determined, self-righteous way to put the question of marriage to me. He caught me out in the garden and told me that though he doesn't at all approve of my pro-Boer stand, and included Dad in his stern disapproval, he was sure that because of my 'fire and energy' I would make an admirable mate, and that he was certain I would find fulfillment in the life of a parson's wife. As he spoke, I could tell how enormously pleased he was with his decision (only arrived at, I'll wager, after weighing every possible consequence), and that he took it for granted he was paying me the most enormous compliment.

"Picture to yourself, then, his reaction when I told him I had other plans. His little gray pebble eyes grew even smaller, and a dew came out on his pallid face and around his pale lips. He smelled damp and his breath, that is always so peculiar—quite indescribable—became so noticeable that I had to step back. But he had a hand clutched around my arm, as he always does when I meet him in the lane by chance and he wants me not to get away, and his clutch tightened.

"If I had some presumptuous notion, he said, that a gardener's daughter had any chance whatever of insinuating her way into the Cames family by way of Andrew Cames, I had better review my own background. I asked what led him to the conclusion that I was bent on insinuation, and he said he was well aware that Andrew Cames and I had played together as children and seen much of each other since, but this was simply idle indulgence on young Cames's part and if his father had been alive, he would have seen to it that the relationship had come to an end long ago.

"He also knew all about the older Mrs. Cames's

tolerant attitude toward me, being as he was in the private confidence of her daughter-in-law. He thought my persistence in taking advantage of the older lady's whims in order to make a place for myself within the family quite shameful, and that the sooner I got it into my head that young Cames would never dream of marrying other than a woman of refinement and education, someone from a family of quality, the better it would be for my own peace of mind.

"I had the most furious impulse to tell him that Dad had studied at Cambridge among other things botany and landscape architecture, that actually he had had a splendid education and that only his inability to take final examinations without becoming ill of nervous exhaustion prevented him from going down with honors. But of course I explained nothing, and never would.

"I shall keep thinking of you. As I must work at something, I am going to paper the dining room with a most beautiful paper I've found, a dull gold background scattered with birds in blue and green rather like the paper in the dining room at Abbotsford. As you have hurt me in the past, so now I've hurt you when I would never have wanted to. Try to understand that I maun do what I maun do—gang my ain gait. Perhaps get into St. Andrews if I can, if they'll have me.

"Keep safe!

"Again—
"Deirdre"

But why had that other Andrew Durrell Cames never gotten his letter; why hadn't it ever been mailed, or perhaps given to the older Mrs. Cames to give to her grandson before he left? Had Deirdre decided in the end that it would be useless to mail it, that there would be no point or comfort in it? But why had she kept it? And how did it happen that it had come down all these years for me to open? I'll never know, but I will keep it too, and one of these days, after I'm gone, all my rubbish will be cleared away and burned, and no doubt this letter will go with the rest unless I have memento-loving offspring.

I stowed it away in my inside breast pocket, then reached for my lunch and ate with relish, yet scarcely thought about what I was eating. And when I went back down over the hills I was seeing Deirdre, my own picture of her, which was very clear for some reason, and trying to realize that I *had* actually heard her voice calling from the dumbwaiter, and that now I knew what I'd almost doubted: I had not created that cry out of my own imagining.

I came down into Howeth Glen and went along the High Street in among the afternoon shoppers and saw a little secondhand bookshop and thought to myself that I would stock up on some paperback mysteries, if they had any paperbacks. I went in expecting, because of the British mysteries I'd read, to find a little dried cricket of a man behind the counter, reading on a stool, but found instead a fat young man who was reading in a wicker easy chair, not behind the counter but out near an oil-burning stove on which a pan of water was steaming. The young man never looked up, but went right on reading.

I saw a trough of paperbacks at the end of one of the dusky aisles and went to it, picked out several and turned away to go back to the counter, when my foot struck a pile of hardcovers sitting at the base of one of the bookstacks. There were piles like that all up and down the shop, so that how was anybody ever to find anything? Probably you didn't. You just explored.

The young man heaved himself out of the old chair that might disintegrate at any moment, reluctantly put down his book, and looked over the mysteries, shook his heavy head, his plump cheeks swaying, and gazed up at me out of his dark, sleepy eyes. "D'you actually want just these?"

"Not particularly. Just picked them at random. Wanted something to read. Anything."

"Tchk! Ah, well, then," and he swept them up and waddled back along the aisle, his large feet in their Arthur Rackham shoes splayed out, and dumped the mysteries back into the trough, coming up at length with five others. "Never," he said "*never* buy just anything to read, not if you can help it. Now, these are five good mysteries. Appreciate how they're put together—appreciate the craft. Doubles the pleasure. My specialty, mysteries are. No extra charge. That'll be 25p." And on being told I'd be walking over to Dunhoweth, the very idea of which seemed to appall him, he got out a wrinkled brown bag of that crisp, thin, shiny paper the British seem to go in for, dumped in the books, twiddled up the corners into two little ears, and when I chuckled, "Now, what brought that on?"

"Toilet paper," I said. "The kind they put out for you in public lavatories."

"Bloody awful!" he cried. "All cruel points and slippery surfaces. An insult to the human body.

51

American tourists should write in to the Queen. Perhaps some attention would be paid." I said I'd try to do just that and was going out the door, hearing the old chair sag and creak, when, "Remember—appreciate the craft!"

"Promise I will—" I called back.

And so I went on down toward the loch, walking in and out of the cloud shadows sweeping over the backs of the hills, saw the minute turrets of the castle with their flags flying, lost sight of them, getting down to the level behind Cames Woods, and soon was crossing the last field where the gate was at the end of the lane. Presently I stood in front of the stone house again.

Deirdre's house, I was certain, Portrero Lodge. She said she'd gone *up* to the greenhouse. But she'd spoken of a garden, and how could there possibly have been a garden? There wasn't room for one. But perhaps in the back, if the present wild growth had been some way from the lodge, or in front, if the lane, then, hadn't come straight past as it did now, but wound off in a curve. Any change would be possible in seventy years. And if a garden, then all these trees wouldn't have been here, blotting out the sun.

I went up the steps and in at the doorless entrance and along the hall, looking in at the rooms on either side. My sneakers made no sound on the ruined floor, but there was the sough of the wind, very small, in the leaves overhead and outside the broken windows. Its wandering airs, brushing the floor, moved the tags of wallpaper that had fallen away.

Perhaps this house had been beautiful once. These had been bedrooms, maybe, on the left, and on my right the large room with the fireplace had been the living room—no, the parlour, they'd have called it. I went in, then on across to the room beyond. As in the others, the paper was peeling from the walls and I went over and pulled off a long, irregular strip and dug my fingernail and pulled off another, then put down my books, got out my penknife and set to work.

Five layers down I found what I was searching for: the paper with the dull gold background and the blue and green birds. Carefully I scraped back the layers until I'd laid bare an area of the gold paper some six or seven inches long, cut into it with the point of my knife and lifted it up bit by bit, frayed, spoiled by paste and damp, but a whole piece. Deirdre had chosen that paper, laid it on the wall and smoothed it while she thought of the letter she'd just written to Andrew. I took out her letter and slipped the wallpaper down among its folded pages, and had a sense of the most incredulous happiness and satisfaction, as if something inevitable had fallen into place and been completed.

CHAPTER

7

When I walked into the main hall of Cames, there was Beth coming out of the passageway that opened into the dining hall at the side. I always afterwards thought of her smile as one of the loveliest things about her: with it she gave me a sense of homecoming as I closed the big door. I felt welcomed and looked-forward-to. "Did you have a satisfying day, then, Andrew?" Her voice was quiet, not lifted in the least.

"Yes. And my lunch—were you afraid I'd starve to death out there in the wilderness?"

She laughed. "But I know boys—I know what they can eat. They come in to help us, you see. We've had a succession, and we never can fill them up." She studied me with her dark eyes. "Did you read your letter? And was it interesting? Would you like to come up and have tea with Jim and me and talk for a bit?"

"You mean into your—?"

"Yes, to our rooms, only not in but up. I thought you might be getting hungry again and you won't be having dinner for hours yet. Go along through here, past the kitchen to the stairs at the end."

"All right—thanks. I'd like something hot to drink, but I'll go up and wash first."

"Or there's a loo right through there, if you like—there under the stairs. Come up whenever you're ready. I'll make coffee." She nodded and turned away.

A loo. I'd never heard a john called a loo, but that's what it turned out to be. As I washed, I thought of my coming into the castle and seeing Beth there smiling at me. Now that Hoagy was gone, when I'd come in from school at home the house would be silent, or there'd be the faint tapping from her study upstairs of my mother's typewriter: *tap, tap,* silence, *tap, tap, tap,* sometimes long silence—then the tapping again.

Yet there used to be times, before Hoagy left for overseas, when I'd come home and Hoagy'd be there and my mother would make coffee and we'd sit in front of the fire on gray Berkeley afternoons and talk—about what, it didn't matter. We chatted, randomly and comfortably, and when I looked back on it, I realized how good it had been. Home *isn't* "the place where they have to take you in." It's where they want to.

Hoagy was away for a year before he came back wounded, then he was home for six months before the end, starting with one month in the hospital. But there was the bitterness and anger before he left, when I was just thirteen, because Dad thought he must do what he saw best to do (but that was because

Dad himself was as wretchedly uncertain about the right or wrong of the matter as Hoagy was). As for my mother, she was never for an instant uncertain about the war, but passionately determined that Hoagy must go up over the border into Canada because the war was wrong, and Hoagy knew, she said, deep inside himself that it was wrong, and therefore it was wrong for him to go.

In the end he went—not north, but overseas. And I couldn't remember having any more talks over coffee in the afternoon, going on about whatever came into our heads the way the three of us used to do. She and I seemed to have lost some easiness of exchange, or maybe I had. Sometimes she would try to talk. In fact, after the accident, during the time of confusion when I was incapable of doing anything, I would wake or come out of the fog, and my mother would be sitting there near the couch where I'd be lying in the living room or in my own room, and when I moved and opened my eyes, she would ask, "What is it, Durry? You were trying to explain something. Can you remember?" But, no, I couldn't. I'd try, but there was that part at the end there that was completely wiped out.

Meanwhile her feeling, her terrible bitterness against my father, went on for having let Hoagy leave without lifting a hand, for not taking advantage of his tortured indecision, for being so blind. And then Dad admitted later: he *had* been blind.

I decided to go upstairs to change my shirt because I thought I must smell like a damp dog. But when I came out of the bedroom and got to the head of the stairs, I went up instead of down without thinking about it. Up, and then up again to the top floor where everything became very irregular with slightly different levels and short stair flights, this way and that. I went along a hall toward where it turned to the left across the front of the castle, and with a kind of tense and heightened expectancy, laid my hand on the knob of a door in the corner that I knew would open into a tower.

And no sooner had I started up the winding, triangular stone steps lighted by long, narrow windows, than I was aware of a sudden leap of the blood so sharp that it sent a stab of pain up through my body, as if all my senses were telling me that I was about to be assaulted from behind. I twisted round, and was astonished to find no one there.

"Andy, Andy—wait for me!" And then the same voice, the child's voice, singing words I'd never heard before in a gay yet minor key,

> There was a wee bit mousikie,
> That lived in Gilberaty, O,
> It couldna get a bite o' cheese,
> For cheetie-pussie-cattie, O.
> It said unto the cheesikie,
> "Oh fain wad I be—"

"Andy, what are you doing, scratching on the window? What have you got there? One of your gran's rings? Listen, I want to ask you something. What's a buggerlugs?"

"Don't *say* that! You're not to say it—"

"But why not? You do—you and Barty—"

"That's different. We're boys. My mother'll know it's true what she thinks—"

"What does she think? She doesn't like me. Anyhow, she's not here, so it doesn't matter. What was it, then?"

"That because—that you're forward and impudent and say things you shouldn't. That you're a tomboy and that you'll be common when you grow up. That you'll—" and here Andy's voice, full of mischief, becomes very Scottish, "that you'll be a coorse quine."

"She never said that! She never did! Your grandmother would be angry. What's a buggerlugs, Andy? What's a coorse quine? Tell me, tell me—or I'll ask her, I'll ask your gran and she'll tell me. Come on, come on—" and the voice dissolved into laughter as if she were tickling and tickling him to make him give in.

Then nothing more—until, in a moment, the light voice singing again,

> It said unto the cheesikie,
> "Oh fain wad I be at ye, O,
> If't were na for the cruel paws
> O' cheetie-pussie-cattie, O."

the words triumphant and full of chuckles, then muffled, as if the two of them were pummeling each other, and Deirdre was still laughing.

I stood there on the stairs, listening, passionately, my whole being gaped wide in order to miss nothing long after the voices ceased: the voices inside myself, inside my own mind, that had been so blazingly clear that I couldn't possibly have ignored or passed them over for my own thoughts. They weren't my own thoughts. Yet it was as if I was listening to a play I myself was making up. But how? I couldn't make up words that were completely strange to me. I hadn't an idea in the world what a "buggerlugs" was, nor a "coorse kwine," nor had I ever, to my knowledge, heard the song about the cheety pussy catty oh.

CHAPTER

8

"So there you are, now, Andrew." As I passed the kitchen, I looked in and saw two or three girls seated on high stools, giggling and chattering at a large table where they were getting vegetables ready for the evening meal. Beth had a full tray, and I took it from her and followed her up a flight of steep stairs that would have been pitch dark except that they were lighted by a single dim bulb hanging from a cavernous height on an infinitely long cord. "Jim and I'll get nothing before maybe ten or ten-thirty tonight," she was saying, "what with all the work between now and then, so we make a good meal in the late afternoon. He'll be along presently. He's up fixing that pesky shower in your bathroom—or maybe it's the two of them. Fortunate he's a dab hand at that sort of thing, isn't it? We'd never manage if he weren't—"

We came into a big, comfortable, cluttered room, twice as large as Dad's and mine, a corner room with tall windows looking out across the loch in one direction and, in the other, up toward the center of Dunhoweth with its clustering of houses where the pier is. I liked the clutter, the atmosphere of peace and comfort and relaxed privacy, the abundance of light. And I felt I was being "let in," as if, already, I belonged.

I noticed at once the silky tabby curled on the old wrinkled, sunken-looking couch in front of the fire, a tabby with white paws and snowy breast and a ridiculous black mustache set slightly askew. "Sophanisba," said Beth, fiddling two piles of *Illustrated London News* and Scottish magazines together to make a level surface on the coffee table so that I could put the tray down. "Or plain Sophie." I sat down on the couch and felt the springs give, and took Sophie onto my lap where she melted down onto her hind legs with her body and front paws resting against my chest and her green eyes blinking into mine.

Stroking her, I said, " 'There was a wee bit mousikie—' but how does it go on? Something about 'It couldna get a bite o' cheese—' "

Beth put a cup of coffee in front of me and stared up in surprise. "How did you know that? I haven't heard it since I was a child, and it hasn't come to mind in all these years."

> There was a wee bit mousikie,
> That lived in Gilberaty, O,

And I took her up, hearing the words sung in a minor key, yet gaily,

> It couldna get a bite o' cheese,
> For cheetie-pussie-cattie, O.
> It said unto the cheesikie,

"Yes, I remember—I remember," Beth exclaimed.

> It said unto the cheesikie,
> "Oh fain wad I be at ye, O,

And I finished,

> If't were na for the cruel paws
> O' cheetie-pussie-cattie, O."

We laughed together, and then Beth sat down and looked at me. "Where did you get it, Andrew? Did your Dad say it to you? Was it in the letter?"

"But didn't you read it?"

"No, oddly enough. I kept meaning to, but then either didn't have the time or couldn't find it."

And now Jim came in and sat down in the big chair near the fireplace where his slippers were, and he talked about the showers and how he'd managed, he hoped, to fix them, but couldn't guarantee, what with the blasted plumbing in general in this castle.

"Jim," said Beth, "what do you suppose? Andrew knows that old rhyme about the cheetie-pussie-cat. D'you remember it? You know, the mousikie that lived in Gilberaty, O."

"Good Lord, I haven't thought o' that in years and years and donkey's years. Wherever did ye hear it, Andrew?"

"Maybe Dad used to say it. He was always telling us, Hoagy and me, things about when he was a kid, coming to the castle for the summer. And about anything 'specially successful or exciting being a real bobby-dazzler."

Jim laughed and slapped his knee. "There's a grand expression, now, isn't it?" he said delightedly.

"Couldn't be said better. A r-real bobby-dazzler!"

And it was on the tip of my tongue to ask about a coorse kwine and what a buggerlugs was, but didn't, and then Beth leaned over and touched my knee.

"Andrew," she said, "I'd like you to understand about Phineas. I saw you took against him instantly when he put out his hand for the letter. It was a nervy thing for him to do, but especially it was the *way* he did it. I'd handed it to you to keep, and I suppose it's that rather bland, imperious way he has with him and the kind of measuring look he sometimes gives people that so often puts them off—"

"It does that, sure enough," Jim said, and looked at the fire, no doubt seeing in his mind the various occasions on which Phineas had put people off. "Now, today, for instance, he'll be instructing your father in the subtleties of golf. I take it your father's an experienced player, with that big bag full o' clubs he's brought with him, and yet Phineas, who's not all that superior himself, will be taking it upon himself to point out gently, in a low voice and in private, in your father's ear, how he might have avoided that last hook if he'd just turned his hands a wee bitty this way or that, or changed his stance, or held the club a bit differently, or stood a bit more over the ball—"

I grinned to myself with pure pleasure, knowing Dad, and picturing his reaction to the Quark's advice.

"For instance, now," said Beth, "there's that nice Professor Fairlie who's the head of Phineas's department—psychology—at the university. He lives across the loch from us and comes over to the castle now and then to bring friends to dinner when he's here from the city. Let me show you, Andrew, where he lives," and we got up from the couch and went around and over to the other side of the room where the windows gave a view of the loch. "See there," and she put her arm around me to turn me in the right direction, "see over there where that gray sort of tower sticks up out of the trees right about the middle. It's not actually a tower, it's just that the house is tall. It's too big, really, for one person now that his wife's gone, but he stays on, with an apartment in the city for when he doesn't have the time to come up.

"But in any case, what I'm leading to—he and Phineas used to play golf weekends, and then it stopped. They just didn't go out together anymore, and we hardly had to wonder why. Professor Fairlie is a quiet man and I have a feeling that if he got fed up with Phineas's instructions, he didn't want to put him in his place but preferred just to have other things to do.

"And it's sad, because I know Phineas worships the man. Well, maybe I should say enormously admires him. He's a hero to Phineas, someone who can do no wrong. So I think it must have been hurtful when they stopped having their weekend golf games, because it was something Phineas always looked forward to."

"You and yer fussing over Phineas!" said Jim. But he wasn't exasperated. Rather, his voice was fond, as if he understood Beth and liked what he understood.

"I don't fuss over him. But life can't be easy for him, what with his mother. You see, Andrew, he lives with his mother. I think he must have a mother-fixation, or some enormous sense of duty toward her. This is the one time he gets away, these three weeks here at Dunhoweth, and then, by heaven, if that woman won't call him up at least once while he's here to tell him she's deathly ill and he must come home immediately—"

"She should be strangled, that one," said Jim.

"And so off he goes, and back he comes in two or three days to report it was nothing, or that she had the sniffles, and all she wants is an excuse to interrupt his holiday. But he goes as if she had him on a string. And the worst part is his *having* to go, knowing perfectly well he's being had, being made a fool of, being humiliated and having to hide it, going off full of sham amusement."

CHAPTER

9

Coming down the stairs from Beth and Jim's rooms, I heard the rattle of clubs in their bags, and the bags being dumped on the floor of the big hall. Dad and Phineas and his friend (yes, his name was Maxwell; that was it) had arrived, and smiling to myself, half with repletion after a good meal, and half with anticipation at taking in the Quark's mood after Dad told him off, I went out to meet them.

I came into the hall and Phineas turned. "There he is, now—the young explorer. Was it a good walk, Andrew, off by your lone?" He seemed not in the least subdued by anything or anyone, if Dad *had* told him to mind his own business.

Dad had been going over the letters on the table, and he turned. "Any mail, Andrew?"

"I don't know. I didn't think to look. Did you have a decent game?"

"Oh, more than decent," Phineas answered. "It was an excellent game. Especially as your father and Eilona trounced us good and proper. I must say your father is quite a passable golfer, though I didn't do too badly, did I, Alec, considering my own partner continually landed in bunkers and ended up each hole two or three over par. No, I think I held up my end very well." He gave a small, self-satisfied chuckle. "Old Max's gone on up, feeling a bit depressed."

"And who's Eilona?" I meant was she a woman or was this a last name.

Dad smiled and I noticed his relaxed and easy mood and knew at once he'd had a good game. "Eilona McKay. Would you believe it—the luck! The fourth in our foursome didn't show up, and here comes this little woman, firm and assured, and asks if we'd mind if she joined us. She said she didn't think we'd regret it because she plays to a six handicap. And you know, she never let me down once. In fact, knowing the course, she saved my hide. By the way, Andrew, do you have anything you'd like to do? I mean anything special? The thing is, we signed up for tomorrow."

"Then what difference does it make what I'd like to do?"

"But *is* there? Would you like to go somewhere? Perhaps the next day? I don't want to leave you hanging around here alone, wishing you were home."

For some reason this sharply annoyed me, it being said in front of the Quark. "I don't wish I was home, and I'm all taken care of."

"Are you, now!" said Phineas, his little eyes behind their thick glasses fixed on me. "And will it be the hills day after day?"

I didn't answer and Dad said, "I was up early this morning wandering around upstairs and in the towers, but it's disheartening seeing all the rooms empty after the way I remember them. I wanted to find my room, the one up at the very top that Aunt Mill always saved for me. I always used to call it the eagle's eyrie. Why don't you go up and have a look, Andrew?"

I turned away and Dad was telling Phineas how the castle used to be. "You can't imagine how beautiful everything was then, the gardens, and how sweeping and smooth the lawns were. I can't believe how the trees have crowded in where the lawns used to be—I can't for the life of me connect, out there, with what I remember—"

They'd picked up their clubs and were coming along behind me, and I lost what Dad was saying, and heard instead, "Andy, what are you doing, scratching on the window? What have you got there? One of your gran's rings?" But not as I'd heard the words this afternoon; I was only remembering, yet they stood out now in my mind with intriguing implication when until this moment I hadn't thought twice about them. I went on up, noticing that Phineas gave me a quick glance. But he was caught in Dad's reminiscing, and I could go alone to the fourth floor and along the hall, and find that corner door again, go into the tower, then up the winding stairs, examining window after window from top to bottom until I found the one I was searching for. Down in the corner—yes, there they were—the scratched initials, very small, D.M. and A.D.C. inside a rather wobbly, curiously shaped circle, as if meaning "We two are one."

At once I felt the same astonished sense of completion I'd had when I went into Portrero Lodge and found the wallpaper, but above all when I'd read Deirdre's words about the dumbwaiter and how she'd called out in terror to Andy to let her out, knowing from her own hand why I'd heard those words just at that place last night.

Dad and Phineas were coming upstairs as I opened the tower door. I stood there with one hand still on the knob, thinking what I would say to Phineas. And the question came as I'd known instantly it would, aware of some interior warning.

"Well, Andrew, and what now?"

"What do you mean, '—and what now?' "

"Yesterday when you were coming up and stopped at the dumbwaiter, I wondered why you stopped so suddenly."

"Only trying to think what I'd done with my book and guessed I must have left it on the train."

"I see. Just now you looked enormously pleased, as if something had happened that you expected to happen."

"Did I? I went up for the view and it's even better than I thought it would be."

When we got back to our room, I asked Dad if there'd been any trouble with Phineas during the day. He smiled. "Phineas started helping me, and I said if he'd tend to his game I'd tend to mine, and that way we'd get along first-rate. I said I was surprised he didn't know better than to offer advice when he hadn't been asked for it. And he said, oh, well, if that was the way I felt, and trotted off like a pup that's been scolded, then two minutes later came back as friendly as ever.

He's an odd little coot, but I think we'll get along."

"Like a pup, you said. But don't fool yourself. He's no pup."

"You don't like him, do you, Andrew? Why not? Because of the letter business? But he doesn't mean anything—he's just curious. Really, he's quite a sympathetic little guy."

I felt the familiar warning signal. "What do you mean—sympathetic?"

"Well, I mentioned about Hoagy, about his not being here—just in the course of the conversation, not going into it. And though he didn't say very much, I had a kind of sense of something from him. I can't explain it. He seemed to understand how you'd be feeling."

"Me! What did I have to do with it?" My voice rose. "You didn't talk about me, did you?"

"No, Andy, I didn't. What's the matter with you? Well, I may have mentioned you'd been through a rough time, but what if I did?"

"What do you mean, what if you did?" My voice cracked the way it would do after it changed whenever I was in an emotional state. "What do you *mean*? I told you last night—lying right here on this bed—I told you not to talk about me to that little nark. He's a prying, nosey bastard and I said, 'Just do me a favor, will you? Just don't talk about me to anyone.' I *said* that, and you heard me. You weren't asleep—"

"All *right,* Andrew, all *right.*" Dad's voice had taken on that awful hushing tone I knew so well and hated because it took me back to that time, as if I'd never left it, right after Hoagy was killed. "Just don't get so worked up—there's no need. We didn't pursue the subject. Nothing else was said, not a word. I don't

70

know why you have this thing about Phineas. What's happened? I've been there at every meeting between the two of you and I can't imagine why you've taken so violently against the man."

"All right, just forget the whole damned thing. Maybe I'm wrong." I flopped back on the bed and closed my eyes. If I shut him out, maybe Dad'd go away.

"I think you're wrong, Andrew, and it's not good for you to get in a state like this. I thought it was all over, that we'd left this kind of thing behind. I'll go and take my shower—why don't you have one?"

He went out and I drew a deep, shaking breath. I didn't want to get into a state. I wanted only to be like I was up in the hills, the way I'd been all day, peaceful and quiet and—yes, happy. It seemed unbelievable. I'd actually been happy!

And now here I was, remembering those warning adrenaline charges that came whenever the Quark would ask one of his sly little questions like, "Oh, were you, now?" or "Is that so?" or "What is it now, Andrew?" Or last night, worst of all, going on about that eidetic image business. Pursuing—the hunter on the trail. The hunting of the Quark. But on the trail of what? What did he suspect me of? What did he want?

Well, whatever it was, he wouldn't get it; he wouldn't find out a thing. *I would not be gotten at*. And right there, as I made myself that promise, Phineas became my enemy before I had the least glimmering of why he was. He was nosey, yes. Phineas annoyed the hell out of me. But I felt something deeper; instinctively I felt it. And whatever that deeper thing was made the Quark my sworn enemy.

Now at last, I thought, I knew exactly how things

71

stood: that we *were* enemies. But I wouldn't let Phineas know that I knew. Oh, no. I'd take up a kind of challenge that was there. I'd be cheerful and relaxed; I would force myself to be, because only in this way could I throw Phineas off. If Phineas suspected me of knowing that *he* knew something he had good cause to be interested in, then he would be assured there was something. Why he was so determinedly curious was another matter. But right now I'd try to thaw out gradually so that I could discover, maybe, just why he was always waiting for the chance to pin me.

I took the letter out of my inner pocket, opened it and drew out the pages. And on the back of the last page I wrote, very lightly in pencil, "August 3, first day here, late afternoon, on the stairs. August 4, afternoon, Portrero Lodge, wallpaper, and in the tower. Late afternoon, tower again, window." Because they were so important to me, I didn't want to lose track of the sequence of events, and I would continue to keep this record.

CHAPTER

10

During dinner Dad didn't mention the Quark or my upset, and we were having a relaxed, easy hour with very little conversation when, just like the evening before, here came Phineas and Maxwell as we were about to start dessert.

What Phineas wanted this time was to know what Dad would think of making other arrangements about the next day: including a friend of Maxwell's in place of Eilona McKay. "Of course we'd ask her first if she minded. But surely she'd understand," Phineas said, "that we'd like a fellow with a low handicap who'll only be here for a day or two. We could give her a ring."

Dad gave him a kind of slow look. "Well, I'll tell you what. I think that's pretty scruffy. Why don't you three go along and get someone else to fill out your foursome and I'll meet Eilona and we'll try to get two others."

"Oh, no, no," Maxwell protested. "We'll let it go as it is. We just wondered what you'd think, Cames."

Now the two of them sat down, with the Quark in the middle of my view again. And the same hot spasm of resentment rose up through my middle, but I calmly finished dessert and gave no sign that I could have kicked him in the shins. He was such an impervious little bugger; took it so for granted that we were just delighted to have the two of them come barging in and sit down without being asked.

The Quark had something else on his mind and it had to do with me. "You know, Andrew," he said, "I've been thinking about that letter of yours. By the way, what is it all about?"

I didn't look at him, but drank my coffee. "Why?" I asked.

Apparently he hadn't expected this kind of response. "Well, I'm just interested, that's all. The whole thing seemed so unlikely."

"It had something to do with the South African War. I couldn't get excited."

"So," said Phineas, "it was a dull letter about the Boer War, or the South African, if you prefer. I find that disappointing. After all the twists of circumstance it went through before finally being put into your hand, it's odd it should turn out to be a dud. It almost seemed as if some purpose were at work—but to no point, from what you say."

I didn't answer, but Dad asked, "What do you mean, 'twists of circumstance'?"

"Well, don't you remember? First of all, Beth tells me, it was written and then never sent. After that it stayed around, somehow or other, for almost a century. And then, out of all the rubbish Millicent Cames left, and I take it there was considerable, Beth McBride plucked out just that one letter to save. Why, I wonder? I must ask her. She didn't know two years ago that you were coming, did she? She didn't know she was saving it for you?"

"No, not then," Dad said.

"So that it seems," Phineas went on, "as if some sort of precognition were at work. She lost it upstairs, found it again, brought it down and misplaced it twice, she told me, and each time it was found, just by chance. It refused to be lost—it was meant for you, Andrew. And, of course, it's suspected that there is no 'just by chance.' There probably are no coincidences, at least not as we think of them. I'd like to read that letter some time, if you wouldn't mind?"

His expression, as he and I looked at each other, expected an answer, and I wouldn't give it.

But all at once Dad leaned forward. "What do you mean, Phineas? What's this about no coincidences? I've experienced dozens of them. So has everyone."

Phineas smiled tolerantly. "Rather, we all think we have. But single coincidences, we begin to suspect, are just the tips of the iceberg that happen to catch our eye." Phineas folded his arms together on the table and settled himself into his chair as if about to launch into a subject he dearly loved. "You see, it's been generally accepted in the past that a series of similar happenings are governed by causal laws. In other words, that they're the results simply of cause and effect as we think of these words within our old idea of a mechanistic universe.

"But the idea of a mechanistic universe is a thing of

75

the past, the whole notion, I mean, that cause and effect are only what they seem to be on the surface. We understand now how shallow that whole conception is. Individual happenings within a series of apparent coincidences, seeming not to be connected by any cause that we can discover, we now think may be signs of a basic principle in nature.

"In other words, Andrew, all of those apparently unconnected coincidences of your letter being lost, and then found again, and then lost and then found, while appearing to be completely separate happenings, are quite possibly connected in some way. And that's why I'm interested in it. I'd like to read it to find out, if I can, what connection there might be between it and your coming to Cames."

"No connection," I said abruptly. "None at all."

"But you, being inside the happening, might not see it."

"I can see what's in front of my nose. It's just a plain boring letter."

"Well, to me it's a fascinating business," Phineas said. "You see, the unconscious mind works outside of our notions of space-time, outside of the physical framework as we think of it, so that precognitive events are quite possibly simultaneous with those they seem, according to our limited vision, to be foretelling. I hope you can persuade your son, Alec, how much the matter of his letter interests me. I can't seem to."

Dad looked at me, slightly smiling, and one thick black brow flicked up and the other down. "I don't know," he said. "I've never been able to do much with him. Shall we go out to the other room and see who's there?"

What he meant was that people staying at the castle and those coming in to have dinner liked to drift into the drawing room afterwards, knowing that sooner or later they'd get into conversation with each other, the golf groups and the travel groups and the local groups separating out at first, then intermingling as at a party, sitting around until, about eleven or so, there were just a few left who hung on until the McBrides chased them out.

As for the Quark, he must have been in his element and was no doubt the last to leave. He probably had few evenings like this at home, or none at all, and I could imagine what a satisfaction it must have been to him to be able to inform so many people on all the different subjects he *could* inform them about. He could advise both the duffers and the experts as to just what was wrong with their golf game. He could hold forth on innumerable facets of science to those with "inquiring minds." And he could inform the tourists passing through precisely what they must not miss in Scotland and just why, with descriptions of each place together with background historical information.

How he must have loathed his poor old mother when she called to tell him that she was once again quite possibly at death's door. He might explain to her about the new concepts, which give promise that everything is going on simultaneously, until he was hoarse, but as far as she was concerned, there was only one way she could go, and that was out. And she wanted her Phineas by her side at the moment of departure.

"Coming in, Andrew?" inquired Phineas when we got to the hall.

"Nope, going up to write letters."

What I did was to spy Sophie lingering around in the upper hall, and when she followed me, we got onto my bed together and I wrote cards to my climbing friends that showed mountains in Scotland (rounded and bare) and to Bob Hoskinson saying that a beautiful silky dame with white feet and a snowy chest and a crooked black mustache was determined to spend the night with me, which was absolutely OK by me. I also wrote this on a card to my mother.

After that, thinking to read, I opened the book, but sat there stroking Sophie until she rumbled, and went over and over in my mind all that the Quark had said about coincidence and space-time and the unconscious mind and Beth's saving the letter for me without knowing why, or that I was coming.

In the middle of the night I woke to find the room dark, Dad snoring, and Sophie curled at my feet. When she sensed I was awake, she gave a little cry in her throat, got up and stretched, and came along the bed still giving her low, questioning cries. When she got up to my chin, she snuggled under and started vibrating again. I fell asleep, deeply content.

CHAPTER

II

I hadn't planned what to do the next day, thinking that sooner or later I'd go off exploring again. But when I got outside, there was Beth getting into the yellow van.

"Hello, Andrew. Want to come along? I'm going into Glensburgh to do the shopping. Jim would do it, but I always have to pick out everything myself."

"OK, and I can load things in the van for you."

"Good! Come on around, then, and hop in."

No sooner had we wound down the drive onto the loch road than I came out with what was in the front of my mind. "Mrs. McBride, I wonder if you can remember—"

"Would you call me Beth? I see no reason why you shouldn't."

"All right, then. Beth. Can you remember why you wanted to save that letter for me out of the pile of stuff you cleaned out of the upstairs rooms when you didn't know I was coming? For some reason the Quark—I mean, Phineas—is determined to get at it, and the only reason I don't give it to him is—well, just because I don't want to, that's all, because it's mine and none of his business. He seems to have some weird purpose in mind. He talks about precognition. Can you remember why you saved it?"

Beth was quiet for a moment. "It's odd," she said finally. "I remember going out with the box of trash to the back where Jim was doing the burning, and I dumped everything out. As I looked down at the old papers, and the old rags from cleaning, and torn-off wallpaper, I spied that name on the letter, Andrew Durrell Cames, and my hand went out. I remember distinctly reaching for it, grabbing it before it could burn, because it looked so clean and compact and untouched. It seemed a crime to burn it. I had to save it, but for what purpose, I had no idea. And when I picked it up it felt firm and fat in my hand as if it were full of all sorts of interesting news. I fully intended to read it—so strange I never got around to doing it.

"I slipped it into my apron pocket and took it upstairs with me and put it in my bureau drawer. Or at least I thought I did. But then, as I told you, when your father wrote a year or so later and said that he was bringing you, his son Andrew, and somewhere, in one of his letters, mentioned that your middle name was Durrell, I remembered. And I went right to the drawer, but it wasn't there.

"I couldn't believe it! I was astounded. And I was determined to find it, absolutely determined, and I hunted everywhere. I can't tell you how almost sick I felt because it was nowhere to be found. You may not believe this, but it was as if it had been given to me for you, and I'd failed you. Isn't that incredible! But so it was. And then when I finally did find it, the most beautiful wave of relief swept over me."

"Where did you find it?"

"Well, now, Andrew, this again you'll find hard to believe. It was in a book—either Jim or I had used it for a bookmark and stuck the book back on the shelf. But neither Jim nor I remember doing this. I can never understand why the actions we want to remember and the thoughts or ideas we especially want not to lose, pop in and out of our minds like rabbits. Like our dreams. The instant we wake up, there they are—or at least the vivid ones. But a few minutes or an hour later, they're gone—simply vanished and not to be recovered."

"And you never read it—"

"No, I was busy and then, of course, forgot it. But after I knew you were coming I felt it wasn't mine to open, somehow. It looked so thick and private, so complete as it was. I wanted you to be the one who would open it and read it. Perhaps a silly notion."

I was silent, turning it all over in my mind. Then, "No wonder the Quark was disappointed when I told him it was dull stuff about the war."

"Perhaps it was," said Beth, smiling, I noticed, but not looking at me, "but *I* think it was something more. And you're right to keep it to yourself, whatever it was about. It's your business and none of mine, *or* his."

Seeing myself in the hills, reading it with my back against the dry stone wall, I thought of Hoagy and

81

what we'd planned to do. I wanted to walk right over to the coast, I told Beth, go on up to the highest point north of the castle again, the hour's walk beyond Howeth Glen, and then turn west from there and hike the thirty or forty miles, whatever it was, to the sea, to the Western Sea. I told her about remembering King Arthur and how the Western Sea had looked to me from up there, a long, thin line of shining water. I had to reach it. Hoagy and I had promised ourselves we would when we came over.

"But you'll go alone, Andrew?"

"Oh, yes. We were going to hike all over the place, staying at youth hostels."

"Will you be all right?" I knew exactly what she meant.

"I think I will. I couldn't have gone off on something we'd planned together right after he was killed, or even six months ago. But I can now."

All the same, something happened that morning that I couldn't understand. In one of the shops, Beth suddenly turned to me, holding out her car keys. "Go and bring the van around for me, will you, Andrew? There'll be a couple of boxes of stuff, and it's parked too far away for us to carry it all—" At once, the most awful surge of misery heaved up inside me. I felt so sick I could have vomited. "But of course," Beth caught herself, "what am I thinking of! You likely wouldn't have a license."

"I don't," I said when I could speak. I leaned an arm on the display case and rested my head on it, and took a deep breath. If only I could be sick, but not all over the floor; not in front of everybody.

"Andrew, what is it? Are you ill? What shall I—?"

"No, it's all right. I'm all right. It's just that I felt weird for a second."

"Look, Mrs. McBride," said the man behind the counter, "I'll send a boy over with you. Andrew here can carry one box and the boy the other. No trouble at all."

And so we got the groceries to the van, and I found I was horribly depressed; not sick any longer, but the aftermath of the misery I'd felt left me feeling beaten. I kept wanting to press my fist against my stomach, which I did several times when Beth wasn't looking, to ease the pain. And I recognized it from when I'd wake up after the accident. There it would be, lying in wait for me to greet me in the morning, or rather it would hit me on first waking, then spread gently down through my intestines like a wash of burning acid. But Hoagy was gone; there was nothing I could do. Why, in that case, was I anxious, I'd ask myself, lying there staring up at the ceiling. What was I anxious about? And no matter how I searched my thoughts, I could find no answer.

Gradually, as we went from one shop to another, the physical misery faded, but the depression stayed; then it too began to fade as the morning passed, until it became a vague shadow hovering over our talk at lunch an hour later.

"What was it, Andrew?" Beth asked. "What happened back there in the shop? Can you tell me?"

"I don't know," I said, and hoped she knew I was telling the truth. "I honestly don't know. But I'm better now." And I really believed I was.

CHAPTER

12

I woke the next morning knowing I must get up at once and go over to Howeth Glen to the bookstore before someone else found what I wanted, or it got lost in that confusion at the back. As I'd picked up the books from the floor after I'd kicked them over, one little one had fallen open, and I'd seen initials written in the margin of the page, D.M.C. and B.C., I could have sworn it. Deirdre Montmorency Cames and Barton Cames. Why did I remember only now?

I set out an hour later and at about ten-thirty got to the bookshop, when I noticed what I hadn't the first time, the words DUNSTAN MCCALLUM, PROP. lettered down in the corner of the front window. Dunstan was waiting on someone and turned as I came in. His eyebrows went up and "Back again!" he exclaimed, seeming pleased. I went off down the aisle and knelt halfway along with as much excitement as if I were about to lay hands on some long-sought rarity.

After I'd kicked them, I'd picked up the books and shoved them in impatiently at random along the lower shelf. I searched and there it was, a small dog-eared volume entitled *Collected Poems* and the author was John Donne. I turned over the pages until I came to the one with D.M.C. and B.C. written in the margin in Deirdre's writing beside:

> So let us melt, and make no noise,
> No tear-floods nor sigh-tempests move;
> 'Twere profanation of our joys
> To tell the laity of our love.

It was "A Valediction Forbidding Mourning."

So, then, I said to myself, they'd married, and loved one another and been happy. The writing was somehow different from the young Deirdre's, so that she'd been older when these initials were written. I turned to the front and found, in quite another hand, "Deirdre from Barty, April 10, 1905." Her birthday, or perhaps their wedding anniversary.

I got up and went to the front and laid my book on the counter. "I'll take it," I said, and there must have been a note of triumph in my voice because Dunstan picked it up and looked at the spine.

"The collected poems of John Donne!" he marveled, pronouncing the name Dunne, and so of course I called it Dunne from that time on. "First you come in and pick out five dim mysteries, not knowing one from another, and say you only wanted something to read, and now you come in full of intent and purpose and busyness and *choose* the poems of Donne!"

"Yes," I said, grinning at him, "and now I have a question or two for you. Have you time to talk?"

"Nothing but. Would you like a cuppa?"

"Well, coffee, do you mean, or tea? I'm not much on tea."

"Coffee it shall be, by all means." And he got out a jar of instant, went around and dragged out another broken-down wicker chair and put it on the other side of the old oil stove where the pan of water still steamed, and made us both cups of very strong, black coffee. Then we sat down and began our first real visit.

"Well, first of all—" I began, but was interrupted.

"Name's Dunstan McCallum," and Dunstan held out a large, soft, well-padded paw. "What's yours?" and when I told him, "Now, then, Andrew," he said, settling comfortably with his cup, "here we go."

"First of all, what's a buggerlugs?"

"A buggerlugs! Oh, my!" Dunstan gave a kind of sad, ironic laugh, very brief. "Well, you know, lugs are ears. And we used to call other kids that when I was little—stupid kids with big ears who were always barging in where they weren't wanted. Kids we wanted to get rid of. 'Get out o' here, buggerlugs,' we'd yell. God, aren't young ones *cruel*?"

He uttered those last words with such passion that despite his "we'd yell" and "kids we wanted to get rid of," I involuntarily saw a huge, fat child with sad eyes, shouted after by other, normal-sized children who hated him because he looked so preposterous, because he couldn't run the way they did, or try to play soccer the way the big fellows did, or in fact do any sports at all, and been the butt of all kinds of ridicule and torture he hadn't any way of avoiding or fighting off. "Get out o' here, buggerlugs," and he was the buggerlugs. And so he'd been left to himself

86

to do nothing but watch, keeping out of the way or going home by himself to read, as he did now, hour after hour. But maybe he was all right as a man because he had the world he'd made for himself.

Yet was he? Perhaps like me he had a wound that wouldn't heal.

"And a coorse kwine?"

"Ah, now that—that's the sort of thing you'd hear out in the little country villages. I don't ever remember hearing it in Glasgow, though maybe in a tough part of the Gorbals they'd use it among the Glesga keelies. The common folk, you might say. But it would be a coarse woman, a coarse queen—loose, someone who'd say or do anything."

So it wasn't "kwine," as I'd pictured it, but "quine." And where had a small boy like Andrew Cames, brought up in a good family, come across an expression like that? A knowing small boy, he must have been, wise in the ways of the world, well aware of how it was run. And if he'd gone on teasing Deirdre like that as they grew up through childhood, no wonder she'd called him rascally.

"Dunstan, do you know anything about a cheety pussy cat who prevented a mouse from getting a cheese in Gilberaty, oh?"

He stared at me. "You ask the damndest questions, especially for a young fellow from America. I've had every sort of question you can imagine—I suppose I'm thought of as the local librarian—but never that one. As it so happens, I have a very nice copy of Walter de la Mare's *Animal Stories* that came in a crate of books I bought not long ago, and I know right where it is. Would you like it?"

"You bet I would. Is it by de la Mare—the rhyme?"

87

"Oh, no. It's old—nobody knows who wrote it, or where it came from. It's just in the folk literature. De la Mare collected what's in the book. Do you know of him?"

"Well, I remember when I was about four or five my mother reading me his poems out of a book she had. She'd just read out of that one book—"

"Ah, yes, *Peacock Pie,* probably. Those are the children's poems. Marvelous man." He thought for a moment, then began in a quiet voice that made the hairs rise along the backs of my arms, speaking almost as if he were making up the lines himself as he went along, reflecting on his own thoughts,

> Sweep thy faint strings, Musician,
> With thy long lean hand;
> Downward the starry tapers burn,
> Sinks soft the waning sand;
> The old hound whimpers couched in sleep,
> The embers smoulder low;
> Across the walls the shadows
> Come, and go.

"Do you see what I mean, Andrew? How he could suggest so much? He gives you what you can't explain. He brings a whole scene before you in just those few words."

So he did. And what I saw was the musicians' gallery at the end of the dining hall at Cames: its walls full of rich colors, trees and mountains and figures and, as I remembered, a glimpse of sea, and all of this lighted by the flames from the candelabra, flames that dipped and wavered and lengthened with the passing currents of air, so that the figures and the leaves on the trees seemed to move as if they were alive. I would go up there and look at them this evening. "Across the walls the shadows come, and go."

Dunstan went and found the copy of *Animal Stories* and turned to the rhyme about the mousikie, and I could see how it pleased him to be challenged and to come up with exactly what was wanted, to be able to trace down some obscure detail out of his vast reading.

"Your mother, now," he said, "with her feeling for de la Mare's poetry—tell me about her." And when he heard that she was a writer and was about to have a book published, he asked about it, and then came out with the fact that he himself was trying to be a writer. And so quite soon it was lunchtime, and we went out and had something to eat—Dunstan a pork pie and I Welsh rarebit, but I was disappointed, having expected something rare instead of melted cheese on toast—and came back and went on talking in between customers until around three or four in the afternoon when I thought I'd better be getting back down to Cames. It was the first time I'd given any idea of where I was staying.

"Oh," said Dunstan, and he looked at me as if I was somehow a different person from what he'd thought. "So you're *that* Cames. One of the castle Cameses. Funny it didn't occur to me."

"Does it matter?"

"Good Lord, no, why should it?"

"Well," I said, "I'll be getting along. But I'll be back. Likely I'll have other things to ask. More silly questions."

"Not silly at all," said Dunstan. "Glad if I could be

of help. Safe home, now. Don't forget your books—
that'll be 75p for the two."

And so I got my books that had been lying on the
counter, put down my money, promised Dunstan
again I'd be back, and went out with Dad's words in
my ears. It was what he always said when friends left
the house, "Safe home, now."

I went to the end of the High Street and out into the
fields thinking of Dunstan, great, strange-looking
fellow that he was with his heavy head and shadowed
eyes, his spotted clothes and ancient Arthur Rackham
shoes with the toes that pointed upward; thought
how much I liked him and how comfortable I was
with him, and so took the wrong path and got into
country I didn't recognize, but kept going downward. And presently the sun was dimmed and I
looked up and saw mist sweeping in from the Western Sea, and remembered how the path I'd taken
toward Howeth Glen, first up, then down into the
glen, had been easterly—not directly north—and so
now tried to keep myself headed in what I thought
must be a slightly westward direction instead of
straight down. But any far-off clump or line of trees I
might have recognized, that would set me straight as
soon as I saw it from a distance, would have been impossible to see now with the mist rolling in, not
thickly, so that I couldn't make out my way directly
ahead, but far objects were lost.

I wasn't aware of how long I'd been walking, making my way down alongside a stone wall, when I
came to a ruin of stones. It didn't occur to me at first
what the ruin meant. It seemed simply a scatter of
boulders that was getting in my way, interrupting my

downward progress. And then I stopped and looked at that ruin when I got close and saw how the wall met one side of it and continued on the other beyond a farther mass of stones.

And I recognized it, and knew what it meant: that it had at one time been the stone house I'd seen in my visitation on the plane.

CHAPTER

13

There was very little left. The walls were down to within a foot of the ground, except the one I'd approached on the north and that still held, brokenly, the lower part of an opening that had once been a window. And it was there, just to the side of that window, that the old man had been kneeling, talking to the girl while he lifted one stone and then another, considering the shape of each one, explaining to her why he chose as he did and what he would do next in the process of mending.

I moved now to where I would have been standing to see it all from the angle of vision I'd had on the plane. There was an opening in the long side of the ruin facing me that must have been the door, and I entered and stood inside the house on its grassy floor and listened. Utter silence. No, not quite. I heard a curlew cry and, far off, the delicate, wandering tinkle of sheep bells. And, what seemed close by, the tearing sound of cattle pulling grass.

I waited, I wasn't sure for what. Did I expect the girl and the old man to speak again, out here in the cottage I'd known I would find? Did I expect the old man to tell me the nickname I'd so incredibly forgotten?

But I heard nothing, and so presently I stepped over the far wall and continued on down a little way in a southwesterly direction, then stopped and turned for a last glimpse of what was left of the cottage. It looked very lonely out there, with the mist drifting over, enclosed in its little gray world as if infinitely remote from all humankind. I tried to take in the full wonder of the fact that I was looking at what I'd first seen on a plane somewhere over Colorado—in my mind, in my imagination—then regretfully turned away.

I had no idea where I was going and was beginning to think I was hopelessly lost and would probably have to spend the night in the hills somewhere. This didn't bother me, except that I knew what Beth and Jim would be feeling, and my father. And then, hadn't I, right in the pit of my stomach, a painful twinge of uneasiness? But about being lost? No, I didn't think it was that. It was the tearing sound.

There had got to be cattle along with that sound, because in my climbs through the fields I had come to know it well. Where there was that sound there were cattle feeding, the black Angus. And now the first large dark form loomed up. It was so big that it must have been a bull, and at once I moved away. Then I saw another form, and another. They were on all

93

sides of me, gazing at me out of the mist—all turned my way.

My heart quickened and I walked on down, avoiding the dark shapes. But they seemed to move with me, and in on me. I stopped and looked back, and all around. There they were, watching me, moving in, drifting, coming closer, coming closer. They would lower their big heads, first one, then another, take a snatch of grass, then look up and chew, consideringly, and move a step closer. Where was the bull? There it was, just there, over on my right, looking at me.

I went cold. The skin all over my body prickled and cold sweat sprang out and began to trickle down inside my shirt and along my arms. But what could I do? Did they intend to close right in? No matter how fast I walked, the cattle were always there, surrounding me. And there was always the bull. The same one? No, how could it be? I must be getting addled with fear. For now I *was* afraid, I had to admit it: because I was lost, because of the gray, drifting, winding, obscuring mist—and because of the cattle. The bull. I had an idea that if I ran I would be finished; I would hear the thunder of hooves behind me and know that I could not outrun a bull.

It was at this moment, when I was coming near to panic, that I first heard the singing, very faintly—there, and then not, and then there again. A song in a minor key, yet not sad. And now I was able to determine that it was coming from behind, over on my right, and drawing nearer. I turned to look back. It would be a girl, of course. It was a girl's voice, though perhaps a tenor might have sounded like that.

Then I saw her emerging from the swirling gray-

94

ness, simply a form at first, then a woman, a young woman, I could see now, in a long skirt that swung around her ankles as she walked down past me on my right, still singing, and without looking at me as if I weren't there, as if I didn't exist for her. Why couldn't I have said something, why not have called out, "Will you tell me where I am? Am I going in the right direction for the castle?" But I never thought of it. I stood watching her as she moved on down through the mist about ten or twelve feet away, listening to her song, words I could not understand (I was sure, when I thought of it afterwards, that she must have been singing in Gaelic), and never said a thing.

As she went down, she gestured the cattle away with a sweep of her arms, first one side and then the other, utterly unafraid. As she passed the bull she reached out and gave him a shove on the brow and he lowered that enormous head of his and turned to one side and ambled off into the mist. "Go on, now—" she cried, and waved off the dark forms as she went by, and they backed away and disappeared. I was left staring at where she could now scarcely be seen, going on rather quickly. At any moment she would be lost to sight.

I hurried after her, just fast enough to keep her in view, though there were times when the mist came between us but I could hear her still, singing that haunting, minor-keyed, yet not sad, song. Then there she would be again, and why I didn't run and catch her up I would never know. Perhaps I felt it would have been useless, that I could never reach her, and I preferred not to test this and be forced to ask myself the unanswerable question.

After another stretch of time during which she

glimmered on ahead and I followed, I discovered that I could no longer hear her and, after the passage of another thick drift of mist, that I had lost her. But now the woods behind Cames, that long expanse, became visible as a kind of tall darkness, and when I knew for certain that this was Cames Woods because of the sound of traffic on the loch road and because I had come to the wall at the back, I climbed over and struck in through the trees and came presently to the wrecked greenhouse.

I looked in through the broken, dirty windows and saw a grotesque jungle of overgrown pots sitting in rows on partially collapsed shelves along the sides and on tables down the center. Some of the plants were dead, but others had swollen to monstrous size and formed a maze of woven, twisted arms that were strangling one another and had reached the ground where they formed a green mat. For some reason it struck me as a horrible sight, all that mad, formless growth, untended, forgotten, left to survive as best it could under the drenching and then intermittent rains that fell through the broken panes of the roof. It smelled fetid, rich, sickening. Underneath the green mat there must have been slime and disintegration of thick plants that could no longer get air and light.

It was somewhere around here, just where I was standing now, near the door, that Deirdre must have stood, about to take in the flats of seedlings when she thought she heard her Andrew call, and turned and looked up, and saw the branch coming down that had smashed the corner of the greenhouse. But of course that corner had long since been repaired.

It had been Deirdre out in the hills.

That had been Deirdre who'd led me down while

she sang and brushed the cattle to one side until they vanished into the mist. I stood by the greenhouse and found that I was shaking. Why hadn't I called to her? Why had I simply followed, having no idea of time, as she went down and down, crossing over walls westerly with a light leap to the top and a swirl of her skirts as she went over? After the cattle disappeared, she had headed straight south while I was taken up with keeping her in sight, wholly absorbed in listening to her and watching the way she walked—that easy, swinging stride that made her skirt sway from side to side, while her hand went up now and then to tuck back a strand of hair under her tam.

Yes, she'd had on a tam that sat like a tilted waffle on her red gold hair. She was the girl who'd knelt by the old man while he explained to her about the building of dry stone walls. The young woman on the hillside had passed me on my right so that I was looking at the left side of her fine-boned face with the straight nose, the slender jaw, her mouth open as she sang, and the clear stretch of her throat revealed, because she was walking with her head held up. She *had* had red gold hair. That I'd noted. And so had the girl by the cottage whose face I'd seen on its right side, the same face. Only that girl had been younger, perhaps twelve or thirteen, with her hair falling down her back from under the tam. And Deirdre on the hillside had had her hair done up, and she would have been, I thought, twenty or twenty-one.

But it could not have been Deirdre. It could not. And yet it had been. And was this any more strange than that I should have heard Deirdre and Andrew telling me, inside my own mind, things I could not otherwise have known?

97

CHAPTER

14

When I came in the door at Cames, I knew the first thing I wanted to do. I stopped at the big table to glance idly over the mail, expecting nothing, and saw a book package addressed to Alec and Andrew Cames, and it was from my mother, and there was a letter from her for Dad. I took the letter and book upstairs, and the moment I sat down on my bed, drew Deirdre's letter from my inside jacket pocket, took out the pages and wrote, underneath my other notations, "August 6, the mist and the cattle and the singing and being led down." I sat there, after I'd written those words, and stared away, going over and over the whole succession of events in my mind, searching for some answer. If it hadn't been Deirdre, then why had she paid no attention to me? Coming down from behind, she would certainly have seen me. There I was, fully in her view as she had been in mine.

Had she known I was lost? Had she been leading me home? Did she know of the situation between us, and what was going on at Cames? Did she know I was the other Andrew who had the letter she'd never sent?

And where was she now? Where had she gone, once she'd seen me safely here?

I never expected to know the answers. I folded her letter and put it back in its envelope and stowed it away again in my inner pocket. Then I went down to the dining hall and up the stairs at the side of the musicians' gallery at the end opposite the big fireplace. I wanted to see those paintings that had reached out to me when I'd first turned and looked up and seen the richly colored foliage and flowers and figures that had seemed so beautiful by candlelight—the candelabra hidden behind the low balustrade so that a glow was sent up from an unseen source.

It was almost dark up there in the gallery on this late gray afternoon, and so I took a folder of matches from my pocket and lighted the candles in the three candelabra, eight candles in each. And when I turned to look, the paintings seemed to have sprung to life in the golden light. As before, the flames dipped and rose and dipped again in the vagrant airs, so that the leaves and figures seemed to move—not when I looked at them straight on, but subtly, when I glanced out of the corner of my eye.

The paintings, I saw, were a series of scenes that unfolded a story. In the beginning, over on my left, a baby is in its cradle and three harsh-faced old women hold up gnarled fingers as if in sorrow, or foreboding, or warning. The mother has covered her face with her hands and the father stretches out an arm as if commanding the old women to be silent.

Now the baby is a young woman with dark hair standing at a window of the castle looking out across the countryside. Her forehead rests against the leaded panes as if she is sick with boredom; the finger of one hand keeps her place in the book she has been reading, or trying to read.

Next there is a wedding: the young woman is being married to a man far too old for her, a king, big and heavy and no doubt heavy-minded, who is staring at her sideways while she turns her head from him, though her left hand is being held in both of his while he puts the ring on her finger. Yet in the next painting, this is not the old king holding her in his arms, but a young man, and they clasp each other and their faces are alight with happiness. Two younger men are with them.

In the painting of the sea, where a ship lies at anchor, the lovers are on horseback, galloping toward it. Then the ship is in full sail with the couple and the young men leaning at the rail and laughing together. Next they are again on horseback riding in woods where sunlight falls on them like bright lace through the leaves and their faces are again full of happiness. Now they are in a small dining room, the lovers lean together in their chairs, his left and her right hands intertwined, while with their free hands they lift glasses as their companions do, perhaps in a toast to the future of all four.

But now they are on the ship again, and are no longer laughing. Rather, their faces are grave and calm, as if they have made a decision and have trust in it. There is no fear in their expressions. But in the next painting they have disembarked; the young woman's husband stands in the background and there are soldiers with tall bows running forward and the girl's lover and his two companions have been shot and are lying at her feet. In the final painting she is stretched on a grave as though she, too, is dead.

I walked back and forth, taking in the story, which I thought I might have heard as a child, but couldn't remember. Hearing footsteps on the stairs, I called out, "Come up and tell me about it," thinking it was Jim or Beth. But it was Phineas.

"Well, now," said Phineas, "I can't believe it—a boy your age interested in something like this. Do you happen to know the legend of Conchobar and Deirdre and her lover, Noisi?"

"Deirdre!" I exclaimed before I could stop myself.

"Why, yes, why shouldn't it have been Deirdre? Do you have a friend of that name? It's the Irish legend. *Deirdre of the Sorrows* was the title one Irish playwright gave it when he turned it to his own use. In fact, several of the Irish playwrights did. You see, here at the beginning the old Weird-women are foretelling the misfortunes of Deirdre's later life, and the father, fearing for his daughter, keeps her shut away so that no harm can come to her. But when he consents to her marrying Conchobar, at that moment she is free to go into the world, and the doom of the Weird-women begins to work. Here, in the next scene, you see her unfaithful, in love with Noisi, and then she escapes with her lover and his two brothers and comes to Scotland, where all four live in happiness until they're beguiled back to Ireland by old

101

Conchobar and his false promises of forgiveness. The three men are killed and Deirdre kills herself on Noisi's grave.

"A tragic tale—and the Irish love it. But then they always revel in a chance to weep and wail and cry *'Ach ae fae!'* or some such barbaric expression, over anything sad and sentimental. And of course cuckoldry usually comes to a dark end.

"By the way, your father won't be back for dinner. He said to tell you that Eilona McKay and some friends of hers asked him to stay and dine with them." I caught the touch of sarcasm in his tone as he spoke the word "dine." "He said not to trouble if he was late."

"I'll likely be asleep. I don't make a habit of keeping watch over my father."

Phineas turned away and then stopped at the head of the stairs. "You'll hate eating by your lone. I always do. Come and sit at our table—there's room. An extra place can be set."

I curdled at the idea. "I don't mind eating by myself—I'd rather."

"But that's ridiculous," said Phineas abruptly. "You just come along." And he went on down and I thought how I couldn't stand his officiousness, this exaggerated concern for my "loneness," which, in any case, I felt was false. And of course there was criticism of Dad in it, when what my father did was none of his business. As far as he was concerned, I knew very well, the matter of dinner was settled. I was to be taken in with Maxwell and the rest of them and they'd talk golf in the most minute detail, or the Quark would start in on me about something, pursuing his purpose of ferreting me out, prying in, trying to get under my shell.

I listened to him going down the stairs, and a remark of his slowly became clear. "By the way, your father won't be back for dinner," he'd said. But what he'd meant was not "By the way," but "And that reminds me—" right after "of course cuckoldry usually comes to a dark end." I wasn't exactly certain what "cuckoldry" meant, but I had an idea.

I blew out the candles and went upstairs to get out Deirdre's letter. There were the words I remembered: "I think there is something up in the musicians' gallery you would especially want to see." And I could picture them later, Andrew's grandmother taking the child Deirdre up into the dark, perhaps giving her a lighted candle so that she could light all the others, then turning her around.

"But why did the wicked king promise Deirdre and her sweetheart they'd be safe when he didn't mean it?"

"Because he was in a rage and had been nursing his rage for a long time. He'd been betrayed, but of course so had Deirdre, made to marry someone she never chose."

"Is this the story of me, because I'm a Deirdre too?"

"No, my honey. This Deirdre is only a legend, a fairy tale. I think she never really lived. Here, let me take your hands. I wish for you a long and satisfying life, and may you and I be friends always, and be happy together for years and years to come."

I could hear them speaking in my mind, see them as they stood together up there in the candlelight, the grandmother leaning over and Deirdre's hands being clasped, her child's face lifted with its expression of trust and content. They must have been friends, I thought, as long as old Mrs. Cames lived. And had Deirdre been happy? She'd seemed to me, up there in the tower, the kind of child who had a gift for happiness. And when Andy was rascally, she had her own way of getting back at him.

But this imagining of mine wasn't like my other experiences: as if the voices were alive in my mind. I was making it all up. Even so, it was strange, because I wasn't the sort, then, to make up stories and conversations—I'd never have thought of "my honey"—yet these words of Deirdre and the grandmother had come as easily and naturally to me as though they had actually been spoken.

I stayed upstairs reading that evening until I supposed the Quark and Maxwell would be through eating and gone into the big room to talk. And when I finally went down, there was Jim saying that Dad was calling on the private phone in the passageway.

"Yes, hullo," I said, inimical, filled with resentment. I was starved for dinner, and the longer I'd waited the angrier I'd got.

"Andrew, I asked Phineas to say I'd phone—that I'll be late."

"He said you told him to tell me you were eating with friends."

"Well, it's all the same. Is there something the matter?"

"Well, it's damned weird, being brought here, then being left to eat by myself. The Quark's insisted on fixing it up so I'll eat with him and Maxwell and their bunch, which means I've had to hang around upstairs waiting so I wouldn't have to."

"Sorry, Andy. Anyway, I won't be late."

"What difference does it make—take your time! I can hear the Quark talking, so maybe they're through, or who knows, maybe they're just going in and I've been waiting around for nothing." I banged up the receiver, then felt hot around the neck, and wondered what Dad would have to say about that when he got back.

CHAPTER

15

An hour later I was playing Scrabble with Phineas.

I'd stopped on my way upstairs after dinner to listen to what was going on in the big room, because three or four men from the Research Installation were discussing time flow with some of the castle guests. I heard the words "moving backwards in time" and, instantly caught, stepped inside. They were talking about the space-time continuum and someone named Minkowski and about space and time vanishing into shadows.

I didn't see Phineas and so I leaned against the wall at one side of the entrance to listen. Now one of the men was talking about a theory that sees the future occurring in various ways instead of in a single predetermined way, which gets around the paradox that foreknowledge of a future event allows interference and changing, so making the precognition false. I was trying to get some hook into this when I felt a presence at my elbow.

"Fascinating, isn't it?" said Phineas. "But confoundedly difficult to understand without some knowledge of quantum theory, which I don't imagine you have, do you, Andrew? No, of course not. How about a game of Scrabble?"

It took me completely by surprise, this question, and I stared at him for a second, at the little blue eyes peering out through the thick lenses with just a hint of challenge in them and more of amusement. I was about to refuse, first of all because he was the Quark, and second because I didn't want to be condescendingly made a fool of. Yes, but I remembered how intensely Hoagy and I used to play—we'd had a tournament that went on intermittently for months—insisting to a grain on no more than three minutes per play by the egg timer and being tyrannical about just what words could be used and what not. "You're not a bad player, Durry, for a kid. Not a bad player at all," Hoagy would say dryly when I occasionally walloped him.

So I shrugged and followed Phineas into the little room beyond the big one where a TV sat, quietly quacking away to itself in a corner, and where there was a table with the Scrabble box on it and a battered old Oxford dictionary and two egg timers. Just like old times, I thought, and knew I wanted to beat Phineas, set him back on his heels, wipe him up—*smash* him!

Another hour later and I hadn't exactly smashed him, but I was about to win. I needed a *u* to go with my *q* and I put out my hand and drew it, then saw with an incredulous spurt of excitement what I could do: finish the game in a way I could never have imagined and hardly dared to carry out. But why not? *Why not?* Just to see what would happen, to watch how Phineas would react, to catch the expression on his face.

I laid out my letters and Phineas looked at the word, without any expression that I could interpret, for a tense little stretch of silence. Why? Because he was astounded at my winning? Or because of the word itself? He ran his hand in one swift swipe through his stiff, gingery hair (he'd done that, I remembered, when we first met, and I'd refused to hand over Deirdre's letter), added fifty-four to my score, then ten onto that, and subtracted ten from his own.

"Well," he said, looking up, still with no particular expression, "you've done it, haven't you, Andrew?" Somehow I had the feeling that he very rarely lost at games like this, games of skill and knowledge, and then only to people of his own degree of cleverness, and never to some high school kid. He sat studying the board for a moment. "And I was going to put *sulk* there, up from the *k,* just to ruin any opportunity for you with that red square. But didn't. Well, we pay for our stupidities, don't we, Andrew? We always pay for our stupidities. By the way," he said abruptly, "do you *know* what a quark *is?*"

I lied and said I didn't, and so got a lecture on elementary particles and Buddhism and the eightfold way that led by degrees to the most minute particles of all: the quarks.

" 'Three quarks for Muster Mark!' " said Phineas.

"James Joyce in *Finnegans Wake*. But there's a German word *quark* which is a dreadful sort of soft cheese. I know it, and it's vile-smelling, I do assure you." He paused in his lecture, continuing to tap his pencil against the end of his stubby nose. "They say, the physicists who're investigating these minute entities, that they're hunting the quark. That's the phrase in use in the physics laboratories. Hunting the quark."

I stared at him, dumbfounded. "Hunting the quark," I repeated in wonderment. "The hunting of the Quark!"

"No, that's not it precisely. That would mean the quark is doing the hunting." We looked at each other for a moment. "I must say," observed Phineas, "you seem far more impressed by all this than I thought you'd be. Are you intrigued by the new hypotheses of physics: anti-matter galaxies, subatomic particles, reverse time flow, and all that? I noticed how intently you were listening to the discussion when I first came in."

"Not 'specially. It was just that 'the hunting of the quark' seems a weird thing for physicists to be saying. But then it's all weird."

"Indeed it is, Andrew. Physics becoming mystical, surrealistic, spreading into the realm of philosophy." He sat there smiling at me. "Well," he said, getting up suddenly, "now at any rate you've learned something," and he tapped me on the shoulder in passing as he went off into the other room, leaving me to put everything away.

I grinned to myself and hauled over the old Oxford. I had a word to look up, "cuckoldry," that Phineas had used at the end of his other lecture, the one on the paintings. There was something that stuck in my mind about that word, regarding Eilona McKay. Here it was:

"*Cuckold.* The reference is supposed to be to the cuckoo's habit of laying its egg in another bird's nest, but in English *cuckold* is not found applied to the adulterer. 1. The husband of an unfaithful wife. *derisory.*" But how did the meaning get turned around? I wondered. Egg, meaning sperm, but the cuckold not the one who left the sperm, but the one whose wife received it. I read on down. Here. "*Cuckoldry,* the making a c. of a husband; the position of a c.*"

But if Eilona was married, my father didn't belong in that kind of picture.

Upstairs in bed, with Sophie curled in the crook of my arm, purring with almost distracting loudness and butting her head into my hand if I stopped stroking her, I'd no sooner started reading than I heard Dad's footsteps in the hall. I'd been going to tell him what the Quark had said, but having looked up "cuckoldry," wasn't sure I wanted to. No, definitely not. Also, I was feeling merry, very pleased with myself, and satisfied. It had been a good triumph.

When Dad came in, we regarded each other for a second or two, assessing moods. "Phineas has been beaten," I said.

"Beaten?"

"Yes, at Scrabble. And it was 'specially nice because I'll bet anything he thought he was going to wipe up the board with me. So I beat him with his own word."

"And what would that be?"

"What *would* it be? The key word."

"Not '*quark!*' "

"Precisely."

"Good Lord! I'd like to have seen his face."

"But you wouldn't have gotten anything. And we don't know what he knows. Actually, he explained to me that quark is a rotten-smelling German cheese, so I guess he doesn't know that we know what we know. But there were signs so I could tell he was burned up at being beaten."

"By a kid of fifteen. How extremely pleasant." Dad came over and picked up the package from his bed and my mother's letter, and sat down and tore it open and read it, then undid the package. "Well, but, Andy," he said, "it's hers," and held up a book. "Her own, just off the press. Weren't you in the least interested?"

"But I never thought—"

I held out my hand to take it, and he ignored it; only shook his head and shrugged as if he gave up. And no sooner had he turned it over and read what was on the back of the jacket, than he exclaimed in astonishment. "I'll be damned," he murmured. "I *will* be damned." He read on in silence, then, "I had no idea," he said, "no idea at all. Living in the same house, yet never to have imagined—"

"You'd never read any of it?"

"Not a word. 'I don't really want to talk about it,' she'd say when I asked. 'It's better all kept in.' " He looked off for a moment, seeming to reflect on how it had been: my mother closeting herself away month after month, and never saying anything or only, on being questioned, that it was a kind of journal.

111

He smoothed his hand over the jacket, opened the book and glanced through, stopping to dip in here and there, then closed it and weighed it in his hand as if its solidity, the very feel of it, gave him great pleasure, a sense of deep satisfaction. His wife had done that. Then he handed it over to me, got his pajamas, and went off to the bathroom.

Her name, Nell Beardsley Cames, was given in full, in letters almost as large as the title, *A Circle of Hours*. The jacket was thick and handsome in glossy black and white, with a pattern in scarlet down the side. On the back were statements by people whose names even I recognized from the world of books, each statement an incredibly (to me) glowing tribute to her powers of observation and depth of thought, to her style, to the play of her imagination over what she had seen and reflected on. From what was said there and on the front and back flaps, I found that this was a journal of one day, the circle of hours from early morning until late night, with time peeled off in layers of reflection so that the whole range of herself as a reading, thinking, feeling, imagining animal was revealed by going down and back instead of along in time through the cycle of the year.

I opened to the flyleaf and found in her unusual, angular hand, "For Alec—from the Quiet One." Yes, that's what he often called her. But no mention of love. What had Dad felt when he read those austere words? Though perhaps they were to be expected (I can say that now, though doubt if I thought of it then) when the final expression of her withdrawal had taken place at the time she started sleeping in her study on the daybed—as though the whole of her life were now being lived and finding fulfillment in that one room.

I turned to the first page and began reading, but after a few minutes gave up and skipped on to passages that caught me when she looked at some scene or phenomenon and described boldly exactly how it had struck her, as if she'd been hit in the solar plexus yet could still find the precise words to express what the sight had meant. Then called on the words of others, novelists, philosophers, scientists, artists, poets, commenting on them to round out the experience to give it an even fuller meaning.

Quickly I leafed through to find mention of myself and Hoagy and Dad, but Dad and I weren't there; only toward the end there was Hoagy, the way he'd looked, his habits of thought and speech, the turns of his humor, always quirky and unexpected, and what my mother had thought and felt when she finally realized he was going of his own accord to take part in something he didn't believe in. Without transition she told of smiting a mosquito with a blow of her hand, then watching it take off again, its flight crumpled and deformed and wavering, but that unimaginably fragile structure still able to become airborne though it had been almost crushed. It wasn't difficult to see the parallel.

Now here was Dad again. I handed him the book and he settled himself with a couple of pillows and began reading. And somehow I slowly became conscious of how he was reading: going on for a paragraph or two, then looking up and thinking, thinking—as if he had something else on his mind and couldn't concentrate, or as if he were connecting the fact of his wife writing like this with something else.

At last he laid the book facedown on his chest, open at where he'd left off, and lay there lost in his thoughts. Because the book bored him?

"*Does* it bore you" I finally asked.

"Not at all. It's quite remarkable—"

"Dad, I'm going away tomorrow."

"Going away? Where?"

"Only over to the coast—walking. Take maybe two days, three at most. Each way, that is."

"But why? Why should you—all alone?"

"But that's the point. Hoagy and I were going to do it if we ever came over, so I'm doing it anyway." I didn't want to say it was a kind of testing, about being alone, to see how I'd weather it, but I thought he'd understand.

"I see. So you wouldn't want me to come. I—I will if you'd like."

It was that minute hesitation, the single repetition of the word "I" that told me how much he didn't really want to go. "No, I'd rather do it alone. And I can sleep at hostels or bed-and-breakfast places."

"Well, phone every evening."

"Pop, I'm fifteen!"

"Yes, well, you phone anyway. And take money. Go into my wallet and get—what'll you need? But take what I have and I'll get more. You don't want to get caught short, even if you think you're going to stay at hostels. And get a good map."

He picked up the book again and went on reading at intervals between staring up to think. And when I turned off my light, he was gazing away at the wall across the room and was so lost in thought he didn't turn to say anything.

114

Later, when it must have been three or four in the morning and I got up to put Sophie out, I stood listening, and knew Dad was lying there in the dark awake, and wondered if he'd slept at all.

CHAPTER

16

There was no likelihood of my starting out. It was thunder that woke me, and the rain lashing in sheets across the tall windows. When I got up to look, I could hardly see the trees of Cames Woods, nothing but a blurred, black mass.

Dad was still asleep. He must have stayed awake most of the night, reading and maybe going over and over whatever had been on his mind.

Jim said, when I went into the breakfast room where Phineas and his friends and one or two others were at their tables, "Well, Andrew, there'll be no starting off now!" And I realized how disappointed I was. I had myself all worked up to go. I'd pictured making off across the hills into unknown territory toward that long line of golden water I'd seen, going on and on until I'd come to the shores of the Western Sea and could say to myself, standing there on the sand, "Well, Hoagy, here we are."

After lunch I put on my jacket and boots, and went off across the grass and down into the lane. When I came to Deirdre's house I turned and went up the steps and in. It was ghastly depressing: the rain had come through leaks in the roof, and puddles stood on the ruined floors that had no doubt been smooth and polished in her time. Long new patches of damp had spread down the tattered wallpaper and something loose banged and banged in the wind.

I went into the parlour and stood there listening and looking. And the familiar tension took hold of me, as if my blood were turned to a different substance, and the hairs rose along the backs of my arms. My breathing became shallow and light, and my whole body became aware, as if every pore were alert. And there they were—the voices.

"—But, Dad, why was it so terrible? I mean beside the awful cold—being there inside Durham Cathedral?"

"Put another log on, Deedee, and I'll tell you—" (That was it, that was it! *Deedee,* the nickname the old man had called her by up in the hills when he was explaining about the wall. But this was not the voice of that old man; it was not her father who'd been up there with her.) "Yes, push the others back a wee bit—careful. Get it on top, at an angle. Now you've got it. Well, the reason it was so terrible was the state of the carved figures on the tombs, the knights and their ladies. They were hacked, as if in a murderous rage—some with their faces hacked off, some their arms and legs so that only the torsos were left. And of course they *had* been hacked in a murderous rage—"

"But why? Who did it?"

"Men who'd been prisoners of Cromwell. He sent

117

three thousand of them to Durham in the autumn of 1650, and they were herded into the cathedral and left there. And it must have been so bitterly cold in that enormous stone place it doesn't bear thinking about. It was those Scotsmen who hacked up the figures on the tombs—the tombs of the Nevilles, in revenge for all that family had done against Scotland."

"But what with, Dad? Surely the English soldiers must have taken everything away from them."

"That's so—I'd never thought. But hack they did. You've only to go and see."

"Well, I won't. I'll never go there. I'll never set foot in England. I hate them. I'd never go to Oxford or Cambridge, even if they'd let me in. I'm going to St. Andrews like Barty and Andrew."

"Are you, then? And how do you know they'll have you? And where would we get the money?"

"Of course they'll have me. I'm as clever as the boys. I can do any of the sums they can, and I've read volumes more. And my French grandmother'll send me. Or if she won't, I'll borrow from Andrew's gran. She's already teaching me Latin and Greek, and then I'll work afterwards and pay her back, and I'll be there at the same time as Barty and—"

The tension snapped. The abnormal awareness was gone instantly. Deirdre's voice ceased as though chopped, because there had been a movement, some movement not of the weather; not wind nor the low rolls of thunder that had been on the edge of my consciousness while Deirdre and her father had been speaking. It was a close little sound, at the back of the house, I thought, like the turning of small stones underfoot, something taken in almost subliminally. And

118

having a knowledge that someone was out there, I turned at once, went into the hall and then right, and without thinking why, to the door at the end which I guessed must be to a bathroom or storage closet. I had to tug at it and for a moment thought it was locked. But when it gave after another frantic tug, I stepped inside, shut the door behind me with a firm pull, and was at once enveloped in close, cold, foul-smelling darkness.

I put a hand on the wall and it was slimed. Should the door be opened by whoever was walking around, I had no idea what I would say. I'd been a fool to shut myself in here. Far better to have been caught out in the open—but why "caught"? Why hide? I had no idea. My action was instinctive and immediate. I just did not want to face Phineas in this particular place and give him a base for his suspicions. This must have been in my mind.

And it *would* be Phineas, I was certain of it. But whoever it was, was now walking slowly along the hall toward the closet, past the bedrooms to the left of the front door and the parlour on the right, then stood for a second or two, perhaps listening. Now a squeaking of the floorboards made me suspect that whoever it was had gone into the parlour. I waited and listened, my body hot and damp and shaking with the pounding of my heart. But why? If I were discovered, I was not about to be murdered. No, but it would be the rank humiliation of being caught by Phineas shut in this closet like a terrified little kid.

I waited—and presently knew that he was standing in the hall again. He stood so long that I wondered if

119

he'd gone, but now he came on toward the closet and presently the knob of the door turned and a very thin slit of light became visible along the top as it was pulled outward, and tugged and tugged. But it did not give. The knob continued to be turned back and forth and it was all I could do to keep from reaching out and pulling with all my strength against Phineas's. But Phineas would have known. And presently I heard him walk away.

There was nothing to do but stay in that foul hole, which I did for fifteen minutes or more that seemed endless, until I could be sure he'd gone; then I shoved against the door and finally forced it open by kicking it. And when it opened I fully expected to see Phineas standing there grinning at me. But he wasn't. The house was empty, and there was no one outside.

I heard the silence weaving itself, humming to itself, except for the soft fall of the rain. And then— two high, shrill voices, the voices of small boys, as if they were running toward the lodge from the gate up at the end of the lane:

> Annecker's sausages are the best—
> In yer belly they do rest!
> Wardel's sausages are the wur-rst—
> In yer belly they do bur-rst!

And then a girl's voice, "But, *Andy,* you said we were going to play spyo—" A bitterly disappointed voice: Deirdre's.

The two boys were laughing, running past, and Andy called back, "Well, we're not. We're going to play peeries—you're no good at peeries—"

"I *am*—I *am*—"

And her voice faded away. And there was the silence again, while I stood listening, listening, waiting for them to come back, Barty and Andrew and Deirdre. But they did not come, and somehow I knew they never would, not on this day; and yet when I went outside at last, I could scarcely believe that the children would not be there, running down to where the lane met the loch road. But there was no one. No one at all. And so I went along under the trees and up the steps back to Cames.

When I went in I saw Dad in the telephone alcove in the hall, and he seemed to be mostly listening. Up on the next floor, as I passed by, Phineas came out of his room looking, as usual, so neat and clean and well dressed in his tweeds and polished shoes and weathered tartan tie in precisely the right shades of brown and grayed turquoise with thin lines of white and subdued red, that it was impossible to imagine he had just now been prowling through the wet around Deirdre's cold, ruined house. For what reason? He nodded pleasantly to me but said nothing and went on downstairs.

And it occurred to me, as I changed out of my wet jeans, that anyone looking in some window of the lodge and seeing me standing there in the parlour listening to a conversation going on so eerily inside my head—a conversation neither remembered nor made up—would have been baffled to understand why I stood so still and, no doubt, I thought, with my head back and possibly my eyes closed. What Deirdre and her father were saying must have taken at least a minute, and there I'd stood, all that time, motionless as if I was mental. I blushed scarlet, watching myself in the mirror over the chest of drawers, and prayed it hadn't been Phineas who'd tugged at the door.

I thought it all over, then sat down on the bed and wrote under the other notations on Deirdre's letter, "August 7, Portrero Lodge," underlining it because I'd heard the voices.

CHAPTER

17

Jim asked us at dinner if he could put an American at our table, and of course Dad said yes. He couldn't very well have refused with the place laid and the stranger standing at a little distance, then looking over and coming toward us as if he hadn't a doubt we'd want him. He sat down and he and Dad began talking, but I paid no attention and looked at my view in which the tops of the trees were being swept violently from side to side in the windy dusk—a rich, deep, jewel-green dusk, just coming on now that the rain had passed, and the stars here and there, very few as yet, were scattered in glittering points.

I'd go out after dinner and the wind would press hard, buffet and slap and whistle in my ears. I could hear it now, keening around the towers of the castle, around the tall chimneys, down the slopes of the roof, and singing at the corners. When I finished, I got up abruptly, excused myself, and left. I went upstairs and got my jacket and, on an impulse, after coming down, crossed into the drawing room to look out over the loch in the green dusk.

Two ships had come in, one an American flattop, now at anchor just below Cames, and the other a British destroyer farther along near the Research Installation, and both were strung with lights that shivered and tossed in gusty sweeps of wind. It was the ships that got the American, who'd come in behind me, started on the war.

Those were a lot of yellowbellies, he said, after he'd gone on for a while about the wooden-headed stupidity of letting civilians have any control over the military, a lot of yellowbellies who'd lit out for Canada. As far as he was concerned, he'd like to see the lot of them behind bars.

I turned and there were Dad and the Quark, listening, and Dad had just started to say something when, staring at the American, I exclaimed in a high, hoarse, and shaking voice, "Yellowbellies! You mean, it was better even if they didn't believe—" and couldn't go on, because I was fifteen and he was a man in his fifties or sixties and he had the words right there to express exactly what he wanted to express because he'd said them so many times and knew what he knew. So did I know what I knew, having talked to Hoagy again and again when he got back, but the heaviness of the man's adulthood was planted there like a mountain in front of me; and the fact of him, and the heat of my emotion, my despair at ever making a person like this understand what I thought and felt and meant, stopped whatever words I might have managed to put together. I was defeated before I could begin.

Hearing Dad speak, the man turned impatiently with an expression of scorn and disgust, and I shoved past Dad and the Quark and went into the hall, over to the door, snatched it open, slammed it behind me, and ran down the steps, along the drive and down between the two high banks to the loch road.

I had no idea where I was going. I only wanted to force my way into the wind, get away from everything Hoagy had told me about the war and what it had done to him. And yet there were the words I'd wanted to say, playing over and over—I couldn't get away from them: You mean it was better, if you didn't believe in a war that ruined the country you were supposed to be trying to save, to go over and shoot up the natives, blow them up, torture and rape them, and call them gooks because you didn't give a damn about them in the first place, than to stand up and say you didn't believe in it and get out. You mean that's yellow. Well, my brother wished he *had* been yellow, if that's what you call it. Because he *went* over, and saw the hypocrisy and heard the lies and saw the vileness—and when he was sent home and got out of the hospital, he said he wished to hell he'd had the guts to face how he really felt, what he really believed, and go up over the border. He said that nobody at home could possibly have any idea—any idea—And then in the midst of all I was trying to tell the American, too late, I realized I was calling him every rotten name I could think of, and that in between these outbursts I was asking in an agonized shout, "What did I do, Hoagy? *What did I do?*" And all the time, because the road was so narrow, I was dodging cars that were coming toward me, their lights shining in my face. "What did I do? For God's sake, tell me what I did!" But by the time I knew what I'd been saying, I had no idea what I'd meant.

When I got halfway or more to the center of Dunhoweth, I turned and went back again and up the drive and around to the rear of Cames because I wasn't ready yet to go in. The dusk had deepened. The wind had risen to an even fiercer fury and the words "gale force" came to me. Branches were twisting overhead, creaking, ploughing up and down. I stood still, listening, and it did me good to hear all that roaring and plunging going on; something vengeful in me was satisfied to hear this chaos of wind and to see the trees so savagely lashed.

Somewhere up ahead of me was the greenhouse, and I thought of Deirdre, coming out in the wild dusk, as she had written in her letter, to take in the flats of seedlings. Now I was at the end of the drive where I could make out the dark bulk of it on its wooded rise and, as I got nearer, saw something glimmer white. A woman was coming toward it under the trees, her skirts whipping back against her and, as she reached it, her hands went up to brush the flying strands of hair out of her eyes and tuck them in. Instantly, with that gesture, I was seeing Deirdre swinging down ahead of me through the mist in the hills, and lifting her hands to tuck in the strands of hair under her tam.

Now she bent to pick up something and I heard the torturous crack and knew instantly what was about to happen. *"Deirdre!"* She looked up, tilted her head back, and I was running, straining to reach her but, as in a dream, seeming to make no progress. *"Deirdre! Deirdre!"* The branch fell between us, smashing the corner of the greenhouse, a branch almost as thick through as my body, and because of its full burden of leaves she was lost to sight. I stumbled my way through it, but when I'd gotten past, there was no one in the blowing confusion on the other side.

I ran up beyond the greenhouse looking for her and calling, but there was no one—no one. Only the sound of the boughs sawing against one another and leaves rushing together, now this way, now that, an uproar cut across by the crack of smaller branches being broken off and falling.

I turned and made my way back, aware that I was tremendously excited about something coming full circle. In the confusion I made no effort to analyze it, but my mind was on it, the fact of it, and I missed my footing crossing over the branch, stumbled and fell and gave myself a sharp stab on the forehead. I heard the Quark's and Dad's voices, then heard Dad say, "Andrew? Are you all right? Do you know you've been gone an hour and a half?" At once I got up, wanting no questions as to where I'd been going and why, up into Cames Woods on a night like this.

I brushed them away and said that I'd stumbled, and went ahead. And when I got up the steps into the hall, I turned and told Dad I was all right, there was nothing to bother about, then went upstairs to our room; and Dad came along directly after and stood there looking at me while I sat down on my bed and pulled off my shoes and socks. Then he undressed and we were both in our beds.

"It's good you let me handle him, Andy—he was a tough one, that fellow you turned on. We both got out of hand, I'm afraid, and of course he didn't change my mind and I didn't change his."

"Guys like that," I said. "Bastards who think they know everything and what should be done with everybody—" But I wanted to leave it. I *had* to leave it, so I took up my book and Dad was quiet. But after a little,

"Andy, I brought you over here with some vague notion of our enjoying ourselves together—going places I remembered from when I was a boy, going over to Edinburgh and seeing the castle and Holyrood and Stirling and Linlithgow. Having good meals at different places. And we haven't done any of that. I've rented a car because there's no use going back and forth on the bus, and I thought we could get away for a few days. We could go over to Arran on the ferry and I could show you Brodick Castle, and we could hike all over the island—the center's fairly mountainous. I haven't even asked how you've been getting on."

"Everything's OK. I've walked up in back of here a couple of times and over to the village and made a friend, a fellow who keeps a bookshop—"

"And Beth says you've been up to their rooms and eaten with them, and gone into town with her to do the shopping. I felt a kind of question somehow, behind what she said, a reproof, as if she wanted to ask why I'd brought you here when I was going to go off all the time. But of course she didn't."

There was nothing I could say because the only remark would have been, "Well, why have you?"

And I didn't care. The reason someone my age had come with his father to Scotland, when ordinarily I'd have been off somewhere during the summer with my own friends, was because I'd thought there might be something to the idea of leaving everything known and unhappy. And there *had* been something to it, far more, I thought, than I'd ever have confessed to anyone.

Now all at once Dad shoved back the covers and swung his legs down and sat on the side of the bed. I thought he was going to the bathroom, but he sat there with my mother's book in his hands and I felt he wanted to talk about something, what he'd been doing, maybe, but somehow it was apparently difficult for him. Therefore it would be very personal and, for some queer reason, because of this, I didn't look at him—because this would have been an encouragement. Just that look might have brought it all spilling out, and I felt—didn't think but felt—that if Dad confessed to me, I might in turn confess, and I knew I mustn't. Under no circumstance. I must keep all that had been happening to me my deepest secret. I couldn't imagine telling any of it; and yet if Dad let the gates down, I myself might say one word, some little thing that would lead to an unwary exchange of confidences. The very atmosphere of confession would betray me into letting down my own guard.

And so I sat there, pretending to be deep in my book, and could feel how Dad was just on the edge of speaking. I could feel him so strongly wanting to speak, and that strong wanting almost drew my eyes to his, but I would not lift my head. I had no idea what I was reading, but I wouldn't turn to him. And presently he gave a sigh, an almost inaudible sigh, and then got back under the covers and lifted his book again. And in a little while I let my own slide to the floor and snapped off the light and turned over, and wouldn't even say "G'night, Pop," for fear those two words might start him talking.

CHAPTER

18

The rain was swept and driven all night long. Even in my sleep I was aware of it, and that I struggled, not physically, but in my mind, and this struggle was so exhausting that I could have cried for mercy, yet I would not let my struggles go.

It's only the space-time continuum, I tried to tell myself. That's the answer. Why couldn't I accept it and let all this searching for an unattainable solution sink away so that I would be left in peace? To be left in peace—not to think anymore! My head was bursting; my very eyeballs ached. If only I could understand about the space-time continuum. Which meant I must get to the bottom; I must explain exactly and clearly to myself just how it was that Deirdre was saved in the past from the falling branch because I, in the future, went out on a night of wind to the greenhouse, having remembered Deirdre writing about this night of wind when she thought her Andrew called to her and looked up and saw the branch falling and darted back. Only it was not her Andrew who had called, but I, a future Andrew.

Because I go up to the greenhouse, she writes about an event that makes me remember to go there because she has written of it. If I hadn't gone, she would never have been saved to write the letter that told me of the event that made me go up and call to her.

Oh, the wicked circle, the wicked, unanswerable, incomprehensible, unbroken circle.

There is no logic, no sense. In what kind of time did these events occur that could make such a circle possible so that I could not determine which came first, her writing, or my calling to her? Each begot the other. I made Deirdre act in her time, and she made me act in mine, and there *could* be no determining which was cause and which effect. Both happenings were cause; both effect.

My brain burned. I needed help and would never get it, because I could never tell anyone of these experiences. They were mine, of my deepest self.

I woke toward morning with my head still bursting and heard the rain blown in occasional gusts against the windows. It was still dark. Dad was sleeping. And the words "space-time continuum" were still in my mind as I lay going over and over all that I had been struggling with during the night. I got up and drew Deirdre's letter out of my jacket pocket, went back to bed with it, and turned on the light. I read over again the part where she had gone out into the windy dusk and had heard someone call her name, had looked up and seen the branch falling and darted back just in time.

"You were nowhere about," she had written, "though I felt very strongly that you had been—no doubt because I'd been thinking about you going away. All the same I thought I had seen someone, whether you or not, just in that flick of a second before the branch smashed into the greenhouse. But of course it was a trick of the shadows, when you can never be certain. It was an uncanny experience, and perhaps my life was saved because I thought I heard you call."

I slipped the letter back into its envelope, turned out the light, and lay there thinking about what she had said. Then slept, with the letter in my hand. And when I drifted toward consciousness again, I had a sense of someone leaning over me and fought to wake myself. Presently I heard a stealthy rustling but could not place its source and was terrified, my terror growing out of the fact that whoever was rustling should not be in this room, and that the rustling would defeat me.

God, if only I could wake up, but it was as if I were trying to pull myself out of quicksand.

After what seemed an infinitude of time I came wholly awake and saw the Quark sitting on Dad's bed turning over the pages of *A Circle of Hours*. I stared at him, at the top of his bowed head. What had he been doing all this time? Just sitting there?

"Where's my father?"

Phineas lifted his eyes and looked at me. I tried to lean up on one elbow, but pain shot through my temple—or, rather, the pain had its root above my right eye, from which point it drilled its way back while spreading lightning shoots all through my brain. I groaned and put a hand over my eyes and came in contact with a large lump on my forehead.

"Feel it?" said Phineas cheerily. "It's horribly black and blue with mauve and chartreuse fringes."

"Where's my father?" I asked again, "and why are you in here?"

Phineas put aside the book, crossed one leg over the other, and clasped his hands around his knees, regarding me with an infuriatingly intimate and comfortable concern.

"I came along to ask after you, after the upset last night and that nasty crack on the head, and met your father coming out to go downstairs. He said you'd had a rough night, tossing around and muttering to yourself. He had to make a phone call so I offered to stay until he got back. He said there was no need but I'm always happy to oblige." Now Phineas leaned forward and folded his arms on his knees.

"You've been through a strange time, Andrew. I don't wonder you turned on the gentleman from America. Of course it was because of your brother, that short emotional outburst and going off as you did, but also—I wonder if you realize it—it was a culmination of the effect on you of the peculiar events you've been undergoing. It came out of the *burden* of them, because naturally you would wonder if you'd been affected in some way by your brother's—"

"What a lot of bilge," I said fiercely, and suffered instantly for my vehemence. I had to wait for a second. "What do you mean—peculiar events?"

"Oh, Andrew, I *think* you understand, though I don't blame you for not wanting to speak of them. They must seem of their very nature to ask for privacy. And yet it would be fatal for you to keep them

134

hidden and unexplained. You've already suffered from Hoagy's death—and now this. I would strongly advise—"

"I don't give a damn what you advise." It was more than I could bear to hear Hoagy spoken of as if Phineas were a friend of the family and had a perfect right. "Just get the hell out and leave me alone."

I heard a creaking of Dad's bed while the Quark apparently readjusted his position. Then there was silence for about three seconds.

"Andrew," he said, "don't put me off without thinking about it. You see, I know that you've been having some rather inexplicable experiences. I *know* this, because I've seen their effect on you and it's my business to understand this sort of thing.

"I saw you on the stairs after you'd newly arrived and were going up to your room that first evening and had your first experience of hearing—what, precisely, of course I can't know. But I expect that at that moment you got your initial involvement with the letter, or with someone having to do with it. You've denied this, as naturally you would, because of the extraordinary nature of what happened. After coming out of the tower, I recall you saying about that incident on the stairs that you'd suddenly remembered leaving your book on the train. Ah, well, now, Andrew!

"As for the letter itself, which, oddly, you refuse to let me see though you say it's of absolutely no importance to you, I've told you of my interest in Beth's peculiar urge to save that particular bit of jetsam out of all the rubbish they cleared up to burn, and I said I believed it was not mere happenstance or coincidence that compelled her to snatch it alone out of the heap. And I told you that a good many of us no longer believe in coincidence.

"Then there was your recital about the building of a dry stone wall. Of course, as I mentioned at the time, you could have read it and then remembered what you'd read—or it could have been an eidetic reading. But I think it was an intense, tranced seeing of the actual operation. What's more, I've found out since that you were exactly right in every smallest detail.

"As for your coming out of the tower, I can hardly describe your expression—one of the utmost satisfaction, as if you'd found precisely what you'd been expecting. Yet why should you have expected them to be there—those initials standing for Deirdre Montmorency and Andrew Durrell Cames? But by this time Deirdre was your center. Therefore, when you went to the lodge and stood there in the main room of it with your head back, listening with your eyes closed, the experience must, again, have had something to do with her. After all, that was her home, and you *were* listening, there could be no mistake about it, though to what I have no idea. And I wondered why, when I went in to say hello, you'd vanished. But we won't pursue that, because it doesn't matter, does it? Possibly you had some reason for not wanting to talk to me.

"Finally, last night, when your father and I went to look for you, he thinking to take his car along the loch road and I to go up the footpath into the hills, and then seeing you heading for the greenhouse, we went after you. I was ahead of your father and I distinctly heard you cry out the name Deirdre at least three times with tremendous urgency, a kind of desperation, as if in warning. And then the branch came down and you went crashing through it as if to see whether whoever it was had been crushed or hurt in any way, and then you came blundering back and fell. And now you lie there and tell me that nothing's been happening to you. Good Lord, Andrew!"

I'd stayed quiet through all this with an arm across my eyes while Phineas summed up the evidence against me. But every time he'd spoken the name Deirdre, I'd wanted to shout, "Shut up—she's got nothing to do with you—don't you dare even mention her name!" like some 1890 melodrama. Which, of course, would have completely given me away.

I lifted my arm a fraction in order to peer out at Phineas, who was looking away with his full lips drawn up, thoughtfully, in the way he would do; then a small, self-satisfied smile made its appearance. Lost, I thought, lost, lost! The only thing Phineas knew nothing about, apparently, was my seeing Deirdre out in the hills and following her down to Cames. But perhaps he knew that too in some devilish way and was simply keeping it to himself for some sly, weasely, beady-eyed little reason of his own.

"All I can say," and I was determined to keep myself perfectly still and low-keyed, "is that you're probably being terribly clever about everything. But you've been wasting your time, Mr. Quark, because I still don't know what you're talking about. Now if you'll just get out, I'd like to sleep—"

The Quark was silent as if cogitating a fresh approach. Then he folded in his lips. "All right, Andrew," he said. "All right, then. But I think you do know what I'm talking about, and you're very mistaken in keeping it all bottled up. I could help you. And I say that you need help, though I'll mention nothing to your father, even though I feel rather strongly that you may need his help too. You don't seem to realize that I'm a friend, not an enemy. I noticed you called me Mr. Quark just now, so that I understand your so carefully weighing the results before putting down the word *quark* the other night. But do you suppose I don't *know* I'm called the Quark?

"There isn't much I don't know about myself. I was so amused when Jim showed you into my room after you'd just arrived and went beet red and looked as if he'd been hit in the solar plexus when you almost let out that he'd already told you my nickname. It was all I could do to keep from laughing in his face.

"Actually, I'd say it seems to be rather an affectionate nickname among those fellows at the Research Installation rather than a derisive or a derogatory one. I believe we're friends, and there's no reason why you and I shouldn't be." I heard the bed creak again as Phineas got up, and I shifted my arm and saw him going out. But he turned at the door. "It would be wise, I think, Andrew," he said quietly, "to accept my help."

After he'd gone, I lay thinking over all he'd said. He knew so much. And there'd been a kind of stubborn, single-minded pressure or urgency in his assault, as if he had some very definite purpose in mind. But what; and why was he so set on "helping"? Why *should* he be so determined to help? Not out of the generosity of his soul—no! He had a purpose that involved my telling him every last thing that had happened and would not rest until he'd screwed out every smallest detail. How could I find out his purpose; how get rid of him? He said he'd say nothing to Dad, though Dad ought to know, and this struck me as a threat. Cooperate, and Phineas would keep quiet. If I didn't, he'd go to my father about it. But how did he know I hadn't already confided in my father? Well, but he could have put his subtle, clever little questions and deduced everything.

But there was something tugging at the back of my mind. He'd let slip one thing—or was it two? He'd said that the initials in the tower were those of Deirdre Montmorency and Andrew Durrell Cames. How had he known those names? Also, he'd spoken of "the lodge" and that it was Deirdre's home, two facts he could only have known from her letter.

The letter! I scrabbled frantically around in the bedclothes searching for it, but it was not there, nor on the floor. But I remembered distinctly that, having turned out the light, I was lying thinking about "the wicked circle" when I must have fallen asleep. I was about to get out of bed and look underneath it when I saw the letter lying on my bedside table. I hadn't put it there. I had gone to sleep holding it in my hands on my chest. Therefore, I must have turned over, let go of it, and it slid to the floor. Phineas had read it.

I put my hands over my eyes; my head pounded because now all at once I saw how neatly I was cornered. If I went on refusing Phineas, he would take Dad into his confidence and the questions would begin, the closing in, the ferreting out—and for my own sake, Phineas would say, for my health's sake. Should I go to Beth and Jim? No, it had to be someone outside, someone impersonal. And I remembered Beth going over to one of the front windows of their big room and pointing out to me where the man lived who was the head of the Quark's department, psychology, at the university. Dr. Fairlie. He used to play golf with the Quark weekends, but no longer. He was across the loch, and the Quark "worshipped" Dr. Fairlie. Wasn't that what Beth had said? And that Dr. Fairlie was a good, kind man. I knew that a launch went back and forth across the loch.

When my father came up again, "Dad, did you happen to read my letter?"

"What letter?"

"The one Beth gave me when I got here. Don't you remember? The one the Quark wanted to read and I wouldn't let him?"

"Oh, that one. No, why on earth should I? I don't even know where it is." Dad put on his jacket then turned and looked at me. "Are you all right? That's an ugly bump you have—it must have ached like sin. You were turning and muttering all night long."

"I'm OK."

"Well, I'm off, then. I've got an errand or two and I want to have the car serviced for our trip tomorrow—or maybe the next day."

CHAPTER

19

Dad had gone, and I pulled on my jeans and shirt and went downstairs barefoot to the telephone alcove. I had to call information because the Dunhoweth book didn't include Burney on the other side of the loch, and when I finally got Dr. Fairlie's number and dialed, the phone rang and rang so long that I was ready to hang up in despair. Finally a low, almost remote voice answered the sixth ring, "This is Robert Fairlie."

I had to clear my throat. "Dr. Fairlie," I began, and was appalled at how hoarse and absurd I sounded. "Dr. Fairlie, my name is Andrew Cames and I'm staying at the castle. You know—the one across—"

"Oh, yes, yes, of course."

"Dr. Fairlie, I'm wondering—that is, if you're not too busy, I was wondering if I could—if I could see you. This morning. If you're not too busy—" My voice was shaking, and there wasn't a thing I could do to control it.

"This morning?" Fairlie seemed surprised. "Well, let me see—I have an appointment in the city this afternoon which would mean my leaving around noon or shortly after. It's now"—and he must have consulted his watch—"it's now five past ten. Did you intend coming immediately?"

"Oh, yes. You see, Dr. Fairlie, it's urgent." Why, when I was nervous, did I keep repeating the other person's name? "I mean, if I possibly could—if you could possibly see me—" I sounded about nine or ten and my voice would go down and become almost inaudible. "I could come right over."

"And it's not a matter we could speak of on the phone?"

"Oh, no—no!" Here my voice, still hoarse, exploded grossly upward. *"No!"*

"Very well, then, Andrew. There's a bus that goes by the castle every twenty minutes. You'd have to catch the next one in order to get the motor launch that crosses the loch every hour. I only hope you can get it without having to wait so long. Oh, by the way, you know, of course, that I'm not a medical doctor."

"Oh, no, no. I mean, I *do* know. I'll leave right away."

I thought Dr. Fairlie said good-bye, but I didn't. I was too busy concentrating on what I must do. In five minutes, in shoes and socks and a decent jacket over the plaid shirt and not-too-clean jeans, I was out on the loch road, and before I had even made it out of the drive and onto the road, I heard the bus rumbling past. I stood there looking after it, then began running. I ran and walked the three miles to the village and saw, ahead of me, the bus passengers getting off at the pier and making for the motor launch waiting for them. By the time I arrived, the launch was pulling away. I ran out to the end of the pier and begged the pierman to signal it back, but the pierman, a big, handsome fellow in boots and thick jacket and with a lock of black hair fallen over one eye, regarded me with a twinkle and said that if he were to make a habit of calling it back for every late customer, the launch would never get across.

"Oh, God!" I could have howled in my defeat.

"Well, look, then, why d'ye not talk to that old fellow over there sitting in his boat. Loder's his name. If it's as critical as all that, maybe he'll row ye across. Only don't let him diddle ye. He will if he can. Don't pay more than 75p at the most."

Loder was a grizzled, shrewd-eyed, tempery-looking old customer, and he studied me up and down insultingly before he answered. He looked up from out of the corner of his eye from where he sat in the weathered old rowboat. "Tha'll be twa pun'," he said softly.

"Two pounds! But the pierman said—"

"McPher-rson," said Loder indifferently, "is the conteenuation of a drunk man's Fallopium chubes. D'ye want to get across, or don't ye?"

Without another word I pulled out my wallet and handed over the two pounds. And when I stepped down into the boat, I saw Loder's lips curl in a mocking smile as he leaned forward to draw the oars toward him. How I hated him. I'd been diddled. I'd

143

been a soft fool. Yet if Loder had asked for five pounds, I'd have paid it.

We started slowly across the loch, across the calm water with the dark bulk of the wooded hills on the far side reflected in the unmoving surface. It had been blue earlier with the sun breaking through and the mist clearing. But now a flat grayness was taking over, a depressing, characterless gray that had nothing to do with the liveness and beauty of moving mist.

I shoved my sleeve back and found it was ten of eleven. Not a chance. We couldn't possibly make the shore under twenty minutes, or even longer, and then I had to find Fairlie's house and we'd have no more than half an hour, if that.

"If you steered over to the west—*that* way, do you think it might be quicker?"

"Aye," said Loder, "an' if yer aunt had pants she'd be yer uncle. There's no tie-up. Can ye not see it's all booshes? Where exactly are ye headed fer?"

"I have an appointment with Dr. Robert Fairlie. You can see his house—" and I pointed over to the right of the town.

The old man's spiky eyebrows shot up like grasshoppers, and his lips among the unshaven growth of dirty gray took on a mincing curve. "An appointment, is it? Wheesht, noo! Ye don't say. An' would ye be gangin' oot fer a perfesser yersel' one o' these days?"

"I'm not gangin' oot fer anything. I just want to talk to him."

"They uni-ver-r-r-sity folk," Loder said acidly, "are a bunch o' cockinchafers."

From that time he ceased to talk and I could see that he was tired: that he was not only an old man, but a weary, hollow old man, and doubted he could get us to the other side under three-quarters of an hour. "How about letting me row for a while—take a load off your back."

Loder stared up in surprised relief, then narrowed his eyes under those incredible brows. "It'll still be twa pun'," he said with suspicion.

And so we changed places, and I rowed as hard and fast as I could, so that by the time we reached the dock I was in a sweat and knew I smelled—in fine shape to present myself to Dr. Fairlie. By the time I'd climbed the hill up to his house, I was even damper and my head was pounding again. As I stood waiting after ringing the bell, I put my hands to my eyes, pressed the heels into them to relieve the ache, and when the door opened, took my hands away and was looking into the face of a tall, thin man with eyebrows as bushy as Loder's but with the kind of expression about the eyes and mouth I would have expected from his voice on the phone.

"Andrew Cames?"

"Yes, sir— I—"

"What a knot you have on your head, lad. Come in—come in. Is your head aching? I shouldn't wonder! We'll get Mrs. Bruce to hunt out some aspirin. Mrs. Bruce?" And Andrew saw a dark head pop out from a doorway farther along the hall. "Mrs. Bruce, some aspirin, please. And tea or coffee, Andrew?"

"Oh, some coffee, please. That would help. I rowed about three-fourths of the way across the loch, and put on speed so I'd have some time here. Loder, the old fellow with the rowboat, looked as if he was about to cave in. I don't know why he thought he was going to get us across. I missed the launch—"

"Ah, I thought something like that had happened. So *you* rowed Loder. A fine turn of events. And I'll wager he charged plenty, you being an American, but at any rate he can use the money, if that's any comfort. Now, Andrew, sit you down right there and so that we'll waste no time, tell me at once what your problem is. Has it to do with that lump on your head?"

"Oh, no. I got that falling last night on a broken branch. What I've—" But here came Mrs. Bruce with a cup of steaming coffee.

"Would ye like a plate of toast, young man?" she asked.

"Oh, my—*toast!*"

"Have ye had no breakfast, then, Andrew?" demanded Dr. Fairlie.

"Oh, that's all—"

"No, no. Mrs. Bruce, how about a couple of boiled eggs and perhaps three or four rashers of bacon? How do you like your eggs, Andrew? Soft, medium, firmish—?"

"Well, medium. But I'm putting you to so much trouble!"

"Och," said Mrs. Bruce, "it's nae trouble. A great lad like yersel' cannae go without breakfast." Off she went.

"Well, now," said Fairlie.

And I thought: here we were in front of the fire; my plan had worked—I had actually carried it out. And suddenly I was comforted, I had hope because I liked Fairlie. I thoroughly, instinctively trusted him.

146

"What I've come to see you about is—is someone you know, Phineas Brock."

"Phineas Brock!" Dr. Fairlie seemed astonished in a quiet way.

"Yes, a friend of yours, I realize. But, you see, he seems to be on my trail. That's the way I think of it—the hunting of the Quark." Immediately I turned scarlet. "Oh, Lord!" I said. "Well, I guess you know that's the way—"

"Oh, yes," said Fairlie, "I know. Don't be disturbed."

"And *he* knows it, and doesn't seem to mind. But I shouldn't have used it. Well, he's haunting me, hunting me, for some crazy reason, and he won't give up, and I wondered if there's any way at all you could get him off my back.

"You see, when I first got here, Mrs. McBride gave me a letter dated 1900. It's addressed to another Andrew Durrell Cames, which is why she thought I should have it. She'd saved it, for some queer reason she can't explain, out of all the rubbish they'd cleared out when they first moved to Cames, long before she ever knew I was coming. And so Mr. Brock's determined to read it but I won't let him. I don't want him to. It's—it's mine. It's private." I went red again, and as on the phone, my voice had gone hoarse with tension and emotion. I cleared my throat.

"Maybe that sounds silly, Dr. Fairlie, but it's the way I feel. He got to me—right off, by seeming to take it for granted he could read it, that I should hand it over. He held out his hand for it—you know the way, like a sergeant major and I was some half-baked little runt of a private." Dr. Fairlie put back his head and gave a bark of laughter. "And then, the first night we were at Cames, I told my father and Phineas and another fellow about how to build dry stone walls. Exactly how. And I guess I did it in a kind of weird way, as if I was seeing it done, and this hit Phineas— how could I know and even he didn't—"

"And how *did* you know, Andrew?"

I looked down and thought for an instant. For the first time it struck me as fully as possible that I couldn't avoid Dr. Fairlie's questions, couldn't lie to him, couldn't refuse to be specific. Otherwise, why had I come? But somehow—*some*how—it hadn't fully taken hold of me that I must either tell Dr. Fairlie everything if I was to convince him about the Quark, or get up, apologize for taking his time, and go. My heart started to thud. I felt rather sick, and it was because of Deirdre. If I told my experiences, all of them, I would be betraying her. I knew I would feel that. I had come to a fatal parting of the ways and could see no alternative to taking the one I'd sworn to myself never to take. Yet if I didn't, it would be the Quark who would take it, start the questions coming, break open the privacy, my secret life, and there would be no going back.

And so, just as a beginning, and not at all settled as to how far something inside myself, my determining self, would allow me to go, I told Dr. Fairlie exactly how I knew about the building of those walls. "It seemed so absolutely natural while it was happening, my seeing this on the plane, that I didn't think anything about it until quite a while afterward. And then while it was happening I felt relaxed and peaceful, almost happy. And it was wonderful after all the—oh, thanks, Mrs. Bruce. This is marvelous." Everything was on a tray which she laid across the arms of my chair in front of me.

She gave me a pat on the shoulder. "Wire in, now," she said. "Ye must be famished."

Dr. Fairlie waited for me to go on. "You'd been unhappy, then, Andrew? That is, upset, perhaps—anything but relaxed and peaceful."

"Well, of course, there'd been Hoagy, my brother, and I'd been thinking about him because of passing over Yosemite—that's a national park. We used to spend vacations there. Hoagy was—was killed in an auto accident. On a mountainside, and I was there right afterward."

"I see." Dr. Fairlie was quiet for a little. "I see. This was recently."

"No, about eight months ago."

"And this experience on the plane was as if you were having a dream?"

"Oh, no, because I wasn't asleep. I could hear my father shifting around and I knew when he took out his earphones. And there was a baby whimpering somewhere behind me."

Dr. Fairlie nodded. "You weren't asleep, and yet on the other hand you weren't fully awake, even though you were aware of your father and his actions. You were having what is called a hypnagogic experience, and these always take place in a state between waking and sleeping, when the body is comfortable, the light is dim or you are in darkness as when you're lying in bed at night just drifting off and letting worries and concerns slide away. Often we drift into fantasy, and that in-between state is the ideal one for hypnagogic voices or patterns or scenes. Perhaps you

149

were thinking of Scotland, imagining how it would be to climb those hills, and perhaps at some time your father had explained to you about dry stone wall building and it all came back—"

"No. He had no idea how they're built. And I've never read about them—never. In fact, I'm sure I'd never even heard of them. It was what Phineas thought, that I'd read it all and that it was—what did he call it—eidetic something."

"Yes, eidetic imagery. You were describing or reading the eidetic image in your mind. And that would be of great interest to him—"

"It would? Why?"

"He decided some time ago to change the subject of his doctoral thesis to—let me think now if I have it just right—'The Continuing Nature of the Eigenlicht, Closed-eye Images, and Eidetic Imagery.' Having to do, you see, with the relationship of a whole range of subjective visual phenomena—unusual and psychologically interesting variations of seeing, of getting patterns of scenes, and these always taking place in a waking or in a half-waking state, like the hypnagogic. So that it's probably just a matter of perfectly understandable interest rather than a haunting, or hunting, as you put it."

I found myself unable to answer, I was so overwhelmed by the mass of explaining still to be done if I were to try to make everything clear with regard to the Quark.

"His doctoral thesis, you said."

"Yes, to be researched and written in order to get his doctorate in psychology."

"So then he's using me!" I burst out, the whole meaning of the Quark's "hunting" at last made clear to me. "Don't you see, Dr. Fairlie, he wants to *use* me—" I understood everything: I was to be his prize specimen, if only he could get me to talk and give him the full story of Deirdre.

"*Use* you—!" Dr. Fairlie seemed appalled, then appeared to think this possibility over very thoroughly. And then it came to me, while he sat there smoothing his hair on one side, smoothing and smoothing it as though not in the least aware of what he was doing, that the Quark's interest wouldn't at all appear to him as a "using" because I'd given him no idea *why* I wanted to keep my experiences private or even that I *wanted* to. "Well," he said finally, "we'll come to that later. Let's continue from where we were. You say there was a conversation in your hypnagogic experience between the girl and the old man. Do you mean you remember a distinct exchange of sentences, as actual conversation?"

"Well, it seems to me I did—yes. He was explaining to the girl why certain things were done and how a wall goes up, but afterwards it seemed to me that I understood a lot more than was actually said. I realized this when I was telling Phineas and Dad and that other fellow about building a wall."

"And the old man's voice—was it his?"

What a strange question! How could I know if it was the old man's voice? But then I remembered that at one point he'd said in a surprisingly youthful tone—and these words I remembered very clearly now that Dr. Fairlie had given me the spur—"But you can't build the wall high enough—you never can. There'll be a crack in it somewhere." I told Fairlie this.

"And was it, by any chance, your voice?"

"Mine!" I stared at him in baffled astonishment, but then thought back. "Yes, I suppose it could have been. I'm not sure how I sound. You know how it is when you hear a tape of yourself. You're always surprised. But I suppose it could have been. It was different from before. That's what I felt."

"I shouldn't be surprised if it *had* been you, Andrew, saying something symbolic, quite possibly of considerable interest to you. I imagine it was a remark quite out of line with the others about the careful building—to last—of that kind of wall. And if you'd only known, you could have asked what was meant. Inside your mind, of course. One can, if one is skilled enough, carry on a conversation with this hypnagogic self, but it's often difficult, I'll admit, if you're inexperienced, to get at the nut of the meaning. Can you think of any way in which that remark of the old man's in your voice could apply to—perhaps your unhappiness and unrest about your brother, for instance? That's the first thing that comes to mind."

"But you can't build the wall high enough—you never can," the old man had said, or I'd thought he was the one. "There'll be a crack in it somewhere." I shook my head. I couldn't see any remote connection between those words and Hoagy's death.

"Has it been a difficult time for you because of the shock?"

Now all at once, with this question of Dr. Fairlie's, I felt that we were on terribly dangerous ground, when all along I'd thought that a betrayal of Deirdre would be the single danger in my conversation with Fairlie. Yet in addition, I could see now what a fool I'd been to think I could appeal to him without devas-

tatingly, at the same time, involving the Quark—
revealing my hand to Phineas through the man I'd
hoped could save me.

"What was that?" I asked in confusion. "I don't—"

"Your brother's death," he said. "Has it been difficult for you because of the shock?"

"Well, yes," I answered slowly, "It hasn't been
easy."

"What has been the main effect on you—that is, if
you'd care to tell me."

I hesitated, trying desperately to see my way.
"Well, really, I—just wanted to ask if you could possibly head off the Qu—— Mr. Brock. I mean, if you
could possibly get him to leave me alone. But, then,
of course, I suppose you'd have to tell him I came to
see you. Oh, God—!" Yes, there it was, the heart of
my danger, and involuntarily I drew a deep shaking
breath and, leaning my elbows on the tray, put my
head in my hands because I had no idea where to turn.
I couldn't imagine any saving solution. Again, as I
had this morning, I felt that I was cornered. Finished.
The Quark would know that everything he suspected
was true: everything about Deirdre, everything about
me.

"But should Mr. Brock even discover what they've
been, Andrew, he can't use your experiences without
your permission and without your parents' consent,
as you're underage. And he must document all evidence in his dissertation. So that I think you have no
need for worry there." But don't you see, Dr. Fairlie,
don't you *see!* I wanted to shout. If he starts telling
my father what he knows, the questions will begin.
And I won't answer—I'll never answer. And the

153

more I refuse to, the worse everything'll get. But I couldn't say this to Fairlie. I wasn't ready to, and I had an idea I'd never be ready to. "Now, about your brother," Fairlie went on. "If you'd care to be specific. But only tell what you want to tell, Andrew. I think perhaps I can help you, and it seems to me you would like to be helped."

"Well," I said, and again drew a deep breath because it was as if I were about to dive off a high cliff, "I have these nightmares—"

"Different—or the same ones all the time?"

"Well, the same idea always, but we're in different places—"

"We?"

"Hoagy and I. And no matter where we are, happy and having a fine time—and this is the sameness—a tidal wave comes in, and I know what's going to happen. Hoagy will go down and be drowned. I struggle, but it's no use. He calls and calls to me as if I'm the swimmer and can save him, when really he's the good swimmer—not me, and then he goes down and I'm always left to find the body and turn it over. I can't tell you how terrible it is—how real, how absolutely real."

Fairlie was quiet, as if waiting. Then, "Is there anything more you remember?"

"No, that's it. They're always the same—the nightmares."

"Then so far we have three occurrences: the traumatic one of your brother's death with the consequent nightmares, the hypnagogic experience later on the plane, and the letter, which Mrs. McBride had saved for you before she knew you were coming. I

154

wonder, Andrew, do you see any connection? Could there possibly be?"

Any connection! Of course there was between the letter and what I saw on the plane. But between the whole experience of Deirdre, and Hoagy's death? Why would there be? How *could* there be? I looked at Dr. Fairlie utterly bewildered and shook my head.

"Have you ever had a hypnagogic experience before?"

Again I shook my head. But wait. "Why, yes. Why, I *have*—about two or three days before Dad and I left for Scotland, I was lying on the couch in the living room. I'd been looking at a magazine and I let it fall and closed my eyes. I wasn't asleep because I could hear my mother typing up in her study and kids shouting in the street. But I saw a meeting—a meeting with a lot of people in a hall sitting on straight-backed chairs—all kinds of chairs, as if they'd been gathered from everywhere, and it was a bare, ugly hall with an upright piano in front. And somebody was making a speech and there was. a big banner nailed up behind him, up high, that said South A——something or other. I couldn't see all of it because of old, faded, dusty bunting hanging down in drapes from the ceiling. I thought it said South America because maybe this was a meeting of South Americans. The audience could see all of it, but I seemed to be up too high so that the bunting got in the way.

"And then there was a thump on the side of the house and I got up to see what it was, and it was only the kids. They'd thrown their ball against the dining room wall and were running off snickering and looking up at me at the window. So then I went back to lie

155

down again and closed my eyes, expecting to go on with the meeting, because I wanted to know what it was all about and what was going to happen. I remember how interested I was. But it was gone, all over. The chairs were empty and turned every which way as if the people had pushed them aside when they were getting out of the rows. The lid over the keys on the piano was down, when it had been up before. There wasn't a soul anywhere, and I don't see how it works: that we can surprise ourselves like that, because, after all, we're making everything happen. I stayed there, lying down, waiting, with my eyes closed, but nothing would come."

"And that's all you remember of the hall? Any more details?" I couldn't think of anything else. "What about the letter, Andrew? Do you see any connection there with that particular hypnagogic experience, or with the one on the plane?" I was silent, trying to bring myself to tell Dr. Fairlie that the child in that scene on the plane was the young woman who had written the letter. "What was the letter about?"

"Well, some of it was about the South African War. A friend of the person who wrote it was going off to fight, and she didn't agree with him."

"You mean the war of 1899 and on. The second Boer War. You said the letter was dated 1900. Could what you saw have been a meeting having to do with the South African War instead of a meeting of South Americans?"

Deirdre going to an anti-war meeting. "Maybe," I said in quiet surprise. "Maybe it could. But, Dr. Fairlie, I didn't even know the letter existed when I had that hypnagogic experience."

"Ah, well, Andrew, there are thousands and thousands of instances of precognition, as in the case, possibly, of Mrs. McBride saving your letter. Of course, we could be entirely mistaken about the notion of a meeting of South Americans having been, in actuality, a meeting having to do with the South African War. However, in connection with this, have you ever had any other experience of precognition?"

Again, as it was apt to do under emotional pressure, my body went hot. The circle—the incomprehensible, endless circle—that I had no way of understanding. I told Dr. Fairlie what Deirdre had said in her letter about going out in the windy dusk to take in the seedlings and thinking she heard her Andrew call out to her, so that she looked up and saw the branch breaking, and stepped back in time, and how, because of reading this, I myself had gone to the greenhouse in the dusk and had seen her and called to her, knowing what was going to happen, so that she stepped back when the branch was coming down.

"And you are actually convinced you saw her, this Deirdre of 1900?"

"Yes—or at least *some*one—"

"There is a great deal you haven't told me, isn't there, Andrew?"

"Yes—"

And all at once Fairlie drew a sharp breath, looked at his watch and then at me. "I've got to go," he said, but all the same he did not go.

"Can you explain it, Dr. Fairlie? Is there any way to explain it—a circle like that, that has no beginning and no end? How can such a thing be? A person could go crazy—"

He was leaning one arm on his crossed knee, the other upright on it, and his hand across his mouth. "There's no use wracking yourself over a thing like that. Live with it, Andrew. Accept it. Take it as a wonder—there's so much we can't explain. However, if the astronomer Jeans is right, about the universe being a great thought rather than a great machine, then it's quite possible that all is coexistent. It's been hard for a good many of us to accept this, but the evidence is there. We must see it. We can't go on closing our minds to it. The thing is, Andrew, we live in a cloud of unknowing and who knows what lies beyond silence? Would you care to see me again, in case I can help? About the nightmares, that is? I think that until you can see over the wall or through the crack in it, you'll continue to have them."

"You think that's what my hypnagogic self was trying to tell me?"

"Perhaps. And I think that you must connect in some way. I think that possibly there is a connecting thread between all the apparently unrelated events you've been experiencing, though what it is, I can't see at present. But I have a feeling it's there. However, Andrew, you must realize that even if you *can* connect, this might not be the end. That is, it would be an intellectual resolution while very possibly you would still have some way to go emotionally." He looked at his watch again and got up, and I went to him and held out my hand. We turned toward the hall and Dr. Fairlie laid an arm lightly along my shoulders. "Does your father know you've come to me?"

"Oh, no. I haven't told him anything about all this, because there'd be questions and carrying-on, and I don't want any of that—not from my family. He thinks I'm foolish to bother about the Quark, so I came to you on purpose because you'd be impersonal."

"You had a rather difficult time after Hoagy's death when there was a good deal of questioning and carrying-on?"

"Yes—"

"Well, we shall see, Andrew. We shall just have to see. Above all, I must think what to do about Mr. Brock's interest in you." Suddenly there were wrinkles at the corners of his eyes and he gave me a quick little grin. "About getting him off your back, as you put it."

"Dad wants to drive around Scotland for several days and we thought we'd do some climbing on an island—Arran, I think it is. Could I call you when I get back?"

"Do indeed. I'll be here. Right now, I can drive you down to the pier and we'll have a bit more talk. Mrs. Bruce—" he called when we came into the hall. And the little dark-haired woman stepped out from a door farther along. "Mrs. Bruce, we're off. I'll be here the day after tomorrow, around noon. Would you have some lunch for me?"

Suddenly remembering, I went and got the tray and took it into the kitchen and thanked her again, and she told me I was a fine lad to think of bringing it.

Fairlie had a little Morris Minor which he backed rapidly out of the garage and whipped around so as to go down the steep drive headfirst. On the way to town he said that it was important that I wait for further recollections and illuminations in a state of re-

159

laxed, open-minded expectancy and that I mustn't work at it. Above all, I mustn't try to force either recollections or solution. When we got to the pier and I stood at the side of the car, he looked up at me and said, "By the way, Andrew, in your walks through the hills, have you ever found the cottage—the one you saw on the plane?"

I found I couldn't answer. Somehow there had been a rightness to that whole thing: the finding of the ruin and then Deirdre as a young woman leading me down through the mist singing her Gaelic song and losing herself from my sight as soon as I recognized Cames Woods, a kind of fulfillment that I knew I couldn't share with anyone. It may or may not have been Deirdre. But no matter who that girl had been, I wanted to keep the experience to myself.

"Ah, well, it's all right," Fairlie said. "I was only thinking of precognition again. But a private possession of the mysterious is very treasurable. And anything you tell me must come naturally—you must want to tell me."

I watched him drive off, saw him lift his hand in a final good-bye. He'd said he looked forward to our meeting again.

CHAPTER

20

I waited for the motor launch in a haze of reflection, not analyzing, but simply going over Dr. Fairlie's words, remembering his kindness, yet with that, his persistence in a way, wanting to get at the effect of Hoagy's death, and there being time to tell him so little, considering all there was to be told; and how, if Dr. Fairlie had been able to stay, what with his perceptions concerning every least detail that brought up question after question, we'd have been talking for the rest of the day and far on into the night; but even so, how he'd opened things out, brought incidents to my mind I'd never realized were there.

Now the launch came chuffing up, discharged its passengers, and the new little crowd climbed down to it. I was glad to go into the dim cabin where there was a bench along each side, so narrow and small a cabin that we sat close together, almost knee to knee, and could warm each other with our animal heat. A wind had sprung up again, not a violent one but fitful and searching and raw.

Why hadn't I told Dr. Fairlie, I was thinking as I sat there, that the Quark had read Deirdre's letter? But that fact had somehow gone astray among the give-and-take of our talk. Yet if I'd wanted to impress on him the Quark's persistence of purpose, his single-minded determination to use me, I couldn't have brought up a better example. And I understood now about my troubled impression of someone standing over me this morning, someone who was hunting for something, and then the sound of rustling, which had so peculiarly terrified me as I was struggling to come fully awake.

The Quark, seeing me apparently deep asleep, must have picked up the letter from the floor where it may have fallen, or possibly even from the bed-clothes—such was his determination to read it—and taken it into the hall, glancing back occasionally, no doubt, to determine if I was waking. If I had been, Phineas would simply have pocketed the letter and come in and talked, deciding later what to do about it. As it was, I hadn't waked, so Phineas had read it out there, rustling the pages as he turned them, then put it back in the envelope and come in and put it on the table. Why there? Why not have dropped it on the floor? No doubt because his innate, almost fanatical neatness must have dictated the table. But I couldn't prove a thing. I could only have told Dr. Fairlie what I thought.

When we got to the Dunhoweth pier, I let most of the passengers get off ahead of me, then went up toward the loch road and back to Cames so thoroughly occupied I never thought to watch out for a bus, but just hiked along and, once, looked up out of my ruminations and there was the bus passing and rumbling on ahead, but I didn't care. I needed to walk—walk fast, so that I made the three miles back to Cames in well under an hour, almost unaware of time passing, and was starved when I got up the drive, up the steps, and into the front hall and then the little side passage.

A girl was in the kitchen doing the lunch dishes; Mrs. McBride, she said, was upstairs if I wanted to ask about something to eat. Should she go and ask? No. And feeling very much a part of the family, I leaped up the stairs and there were Beth and Sophie. And fifteen minutes later I was having lunch in front of the fire, talking to Beth, perfectly content, telling her about the American last night and how I'd gone out along by the loch and then up to the greenhouse to walk off my rage and got hit on the forehead when I fell on a broken branch.

It was good to sit there with Sophie rumbling under my hand and Beth listening in that absorbed way she had. I told her I'd gone over to Burney—though not why—and she enormously relished the story of my adventure with Loder and the idea of my paying two pounds for the privilege of rowing the old rascal across. I found I remembered almost to a word, almost to the exact tone, Loder's remarks, and brought them all off to my own satisfaction, egged on by Beth's laughter and the delight in her eyes.

Dad and I had dinner that night with no third at our table, and the Quark and Maxwell weren't at theirs. When Dad asked what I'd done with my day, I repeated the bare fact that I'd crossed to Burney, but decided not to go into the story of Loder for fear of being questioned as to the necessity of paying two pounds for a "pointless" trip and having discovered, from past experience, that if I put on a good performance the first time, as I had with Beth, the next would be second-rate.

Afterwards, Dad stayed in the drawing room talking to some people who'd sat at a table near us, and I went into the small room beyond to watch an hour and a half of Edith Piaf on television, living her melancholy life with her, that magnetic little being, and listening to her sad, throbbing, sensual songs, feeling I was back with Sheila, and then, just as it was over, knowing it had been Deirdre's face I'd been seeing.

The news came on and I was aware of someone standing behind my chair and I looked around and it was the Quark, with his hand on the back of it. "Hello, Andrew," he said, but I didn't answer.

We watched in silence while the newscaster spoke about war and politics, by-elections in Britain and what Labor was doing and what the prime minister was saying, and then, just as the next item was beginning, Phineas began to explain something, so that a good bit of the first part was lost.

I shut him out and heard, "Continual controversy for the past three years over the expense of having this dangerous, narrow, winding road, on which so many accidents have taken place, widened and straightened has prevented the job being done. Only this afternoon, Professor Robert Fairlie, head of the psychology department at the university, was killed in a motor accident while driving on the Stonemill Road.

A rented car, driven by a tourist on the wrong side, crashed into Fairlie's car head-on as he rounded a curve. The driver of the other car was also killed. Funeral services have not yet been arranged, but there will be a memorial ceremony on Wednesday of next week at the university, where he was much admired and respected. He had taught there for the past twenty years, and had been head of his department for the last eight."

At the words "killed in a motor accident," I heard a most terrible "A-a-ah!" from Phineas, as if he had been knifed in the stomach; yet I couldn't turn, compelled to keep listening to what I could not believe. And when the newscaster had finished, I got up, but Phineas was gone. I saw him walking off through the drawing room that was empty now, noticed how he held his arms out from his sides as though to balance himself as if he were blind, and that his steps were irregular as though he hardly knew where he was going. I followed, and in the hall saw him weaving his way to the back to go upstairs. In a state of shock myself, I stood there thinking of how I had been going to tell Dr. Fairlie everything, and now I couldn't—and so could never tell anyone.

Beth came out from the hall leading to the kitchen, and Jim was behind her. He had been upstairs watching and, the moment he heard, came down to let Beth know what had happened.

"Poor Phineas," she said. "Oh, poor Phineas, I must go up to him," and Jim and I followed, but when we got upstairs there was no answer to Beth's knock. We stood there and caught the muffled sound of what must have been crying, and there were words

165

as though Phineas was repeating something over and over.

Beth shook her head and motioned us away, and when we had gone down again, she said, "He loved Professor Fairlie as if he'd been his son. But it was more than that. Phineas has been an instructor only because of him, rather under his wing, you might say. I mean, able to stay only because of him. Phineas needs his doctorate and wouldn't ordinarily be teaching without it—not at the university. Apparently he's an excellent teacher, lively and imaginative, and the students enjoy him. I suppose as an instructor he's far better than a good many of the old stodges, but that doesn't help him as far as his doctorate's concerned. He's been working away at his thesis for what seems to me ages—always dissatisfied with it, for some reason. And the man who'll probably succeed as head of the department will have no mercy on Phineas. I've heard he thinks him cheeky and presumptuous, so I'm certain Phineas'll have no hope of staying on."

"Professor" Fairlie. And I'd called him "Doctor" the whole time, and of course he hadn't said anything.

Beth made some other remark, but as we stood there, I could think only of how I was perhaps the last person to have talked to him and how kind he had been in every way. And then how contrary and confusing human nature can be, because I had no idea in the world what to make of Phineas.

In fact, I've often thought how I'd hated him—bitterly hated him! And so had been incapable of seeing him as anything but a cold, calculating, impervious little manipulator for his own ends. And he *was* that—he *was*. And yet he must have loved Robert Fairlie. Or was it actually, this intense grief and despair, that he had lost all hope of ever being able to stay on at the university, under his wing, enjoying his friendship and confidence and support? But I can't imagine that Phineas would have cried, as I heard him crying the night of Fairlie's death, over frustrated ambition. No, I can only think he must genuinely have loved the man.

CHAPTER

21

Phineas had packed up and left before Dad and I got down to breakfast the next morning.

When we got back four days later, having done all the things we'd had in mind to do, I was sitting at our table in the evening alone because Dad had been called to the phone in the main hall. And here came Jim to tell me that I was wanted on the other phone, the one at a little cluttered desk just outside the kitchen, where calls came in for reservations for dinner.

"It's your mother, Andrew. She asked for your father, but when I told her he was on the other phone, she said she'd like to speak to you."

I got up and followed Jim out, going through the door that led directly to the kitchen. I felt vaguely disturbed, almost depressed. What could have happened that she would want to phone? But she sounded happy for the first time I could remember in over two years, happy and excited. She wanted to know how we were and would we be willing to come home early.

"You got the book, Andrew? Isn't it beautiful? Have you had a chance to look it over? The thing is, the publishers are giving me a party at the end of next week, and I thought maybe you'd both like to be there. It would mean coming back only a few days ahead of time and it would be perfect if you could be there. Would you mind leaving early? They can't put off the party because they want to give it on the day of publication."

On the day of publication? I didn't understand. "But isn't it already published?" After all, we had a copy.

"Oh, Durry," and she laughed, sounding young and joyful. "It's between covers but it isn't officially 'out' until a certain date, and that's what we're talking about. Will you come?" I couldn't seem to answer, and she went on, "Of course the party'll be in New York, so you'd get your tickets changed to go to Kennedy instead of to San Francisco, and then we'd decide when we wanted to go home. We might even have a little vacation together in New York. Wouldn't it be fun!"

This was someone so different from the person I'd lived with I couldn't believe it. But I realized I felt broken into, disrupted, as if I'd built up, already—within the space of almost two weeks—a life I wanted to go on with rather than return to the old, unhappy associations at home.

I had no idea how to answer that exclamation, "Wouldn't it be fun!" put with such zest and eagerness. I managed to tell her how pleased I was for her; that it was marvelous, everything that had happened. But then I had to tell her that I didn't want to go back, not right now; that I wanted to stay here and try going to school and working for the McBrides and living at Cames, then go to St. Andrews. "I think I'm better off here, Mom. I *have* been better. You wouldn't believe it."

My mother didn't speak for a second or two, as if she were trying to get her bearings. "But, Andrew—I don't understand—"

And then Dad came in, and I told her he was here and he took the receiver. "Hello, Nell," he said, then was quiet while she explained. "Nell, listen to me—listen—" he said after a little, as if he couldn't bear to hear her going on about plans that hadn't any relation to his own, that were, in fact, as I found out later, completely contrary to them. "Nell, I think I won't come to the party. No, no, of course it isn't retaliation. And I don't want to talk about it here on the phone. It's damned awkward—" and so it was, with Jim and the two busboys continually going back and forth between the kitchen and the dining hall, and here Dad and I were, caught in between, humiliatingly underfoot. "I wrote you a letter the other night, explaining everything—"

"Explaining *what?*" I could imagine my mother demanding at the other end, incredulous.

"About my thinking. But at least let me get you on the hall phone—" Another interruption. And then, because she had never been able to brook any delay in knowing the worst, "Well, then, Nell, if you insist on my saying it now, I want to make a change." He was speaking as low as possible, trying desperately to be private, but neither Jim nor the boys were there at the moment, or he'd never have said those words. "Yes, that's what I mean, change my life; but I've got to think—that's why I want to stay here and be quiet." Again my mother spoke. "No, it's nothing like that. I'll be home when we planned, and I'm sorry about the party. Yes, of course Andrew'll be there. And my letter should arrive in a few days. Wouldn't you like me to call you on the other phone?"

No, apparently not. Apparently she didn't want to say any more at present. "All right, then. Yes, I'll tell him. Good-bye."

He hung up and stood there staring at the wall, then turned and looked at me. "She said she'd call later where you're to meet her in New York. It would have to happen like this, just when she's happy for the first time since—and I didn't even tell her how much I like her book!" He stopped, because now Jim came through and hurried into the kitchen, but stood there a moment longer, still frozen in his confused thoughts. Then, finally, "I've got to call her back about the book. It's not fair. I've got to tell her what I feel."

That was typical of him—it *is* typical—that no matter what throes he goes through, no matter what his emotions at the time, he ends up wanting to be fair. And it was because of this that my parents' marriage wasn't dissolved until the next year, when he came back to Scotland and married Eilona. I knew later that if I'd been older and could have said to him about my mother, "But she sounded so happy before you said you wanted to change your life, perhaps everything

171

could be different from now on, maybe worked out in some way," he'd have answered, "I'm afraid, Andy, it's got nothing to do with me, this happiness. It's because of her success. Her work—that's the center of her life, the writing, the new book coming along. It'll always be that. I'm on the margin—"

But I didn't really understand at the time what was implied in that strange conversation on the phone in the little passageway, and when Dad came upstairs my only thought was to find out why I must go to the party in New York when he needn't.

"I want you to go, Andy," he said. "Let's not make a big thing of it—it'll be almost time for you to go home anyway. And it wouldn't be a good idea for you to go to school over here, not yet, not after the bad time you've been through. Finish out your three years at home; then maybe St. Andrews would work out. And come on back next summer, if you want, if the McBrides like the idea. But let's not go on now about the party."

CHAPTER

22

Jim sent me off on my hike to the sea with an early breakfast—"I've a wheen o' wur-rk to do anyway," he said, "an' it's no trouble"—and made me a huge lunch so that if I was out in the wilds at evening, I'd be sure to have enough.

I reached the outskirts of Howeth Glen around eight-thirty but went on up past it. If I stopped to have coffee with Dunstan, I'd never get away, so I kept climbing until I reached the heights and the place where I'd eaten lunch on that first day I came up, leaning against this very wall and looking out over the descending slopes to where, forty or more miles away, the Western Sea shone in that glinting line.

Gradually, as I climbed, the sun had been dissolving the grayness, but still, now, the Western Sea was hidden. I sat down to have an apple and thought about Deirdre and wished she would speak to me. I got out her letter and held it, thinking that if I closed my eyes and saw her vividly enough, I could conjure her. But she'd never come at my bidding—I knew that. I held my breath to listen for the high, clear voices of children calling to one another, playing hide-and-seek (was *that* spyo?), racing each other, arguing and forgetting their arguments, teasing, telling stories when they'd settle somewhere to have their lunches, as big as mine, bread and jelly, buttered bannocks, and cheese and apples and oranges. But there was only the quiet sweep of the wind across the grass and the cries of curlews and skylarks and the plaintive cries of peewits that again and again call their own name. I ate my apple and watched the shine of the sea become faintly, and then more clearly, visible as the sun broke through and the mists melted away. And when I got up to go, there it lay, silvery, a very thin line far, far off.

Two days later, around eight in the evening, I reached it, having traveled down through tumbled stretches of upland pasture, quiet valleys where I sometimes saw no more than a single dwelling, along the banks of small lochs and past tracts of woodland and occasional villages, at a steady, swinging pace that ate up the distance as easily as when Hoagy and I and the others would take off into the high country above Yosemite with our backpacks and go for as long as we felt like walking, and sleep out under the sky.

The first night I'd stayed at a hostel and the second night slept on the ground in my sleeping bag on the edge of a forest near a farmhouse, and bought my breakfast there in the morning. Tonight I'd be sleeping on the beach, I thought, as I crossed a broad field that sloped down to a rough pebble strand where the waves were coming in.

An island lay out there, maybe four or five miles away, and weather was going on over it. In the evening light it looked blue, or rather from moment to moment it changed from shades of blue to lavender between long misty curtains of rain that were sweeping across it. Then the wind blew them past and the sun, sinking molten into the sea, peered out beneath a low bank of cloud across the purple water so that now the island was black against the brilliance behind it. I turned to look at the land behind me and it had gone all velvety: stands of dark trees, stretches of heather and bracken beyond the meadow, and the meadow itself, given depth by that rich, level light.

I moved down onto the beach and stood there watching. Spent waves creamed over the pebbles and drew back, turning the pebbles over and over with a soft whispering. Shore birds with long bills and long legs wandered in the surf, and a group of sea gulls stood with their breasts to the sun, quietly watching its arc shrink and vanish.

"Here we are, Hoagy," I said. "Here we finally are," and felt peaceful and happy as long as I refused to let myself think how much better it would have been if he were there.

At this time I heard a pure, clear thread of sound blown to me from across the water, now faint, then lost entirely, now suddenly distinct, then faint again: a bagpipe, of course, a single piper playing a pibroch, slow and stately, and I could imagine him in his kilt, the kilt swaying from side to side, as he walked around whatever house there was on the island, piping in the hour of the evening meal.

I settled myself on a smooth stretch up near the bank, safely out of reach of high tide, and got out my own meal—scones I'd bought in the village where I'd eaten lunch, a slice of cheese, a couple of small mutton pies, some little sweet-tart Scottish tomatoes, and a thick piece of Dundee cake, full of almonds and raisins and currants.

By the time I was full and sighing with satisfaction, the light had changed and the sky had darkened to its powerful evening blue. Two lights, one low, one high up, were shining through the trees on the dark mass of the island. There must have been trees because the lights winked as though through boughs being swept back and forth. I made a body-sized hollow for myself, got out my sleeping bag, zipped myself into it, and was asleep in two minutes.

And woke in a cold sweat at the sound of the surf. The tide had turned and its deep undertone had penetrated my sleep to the point where, in my subconscious, I associated that particular note with my nightmares and drowning and finding Hoagy on the sand. But even at high tide the waves hadn't come near, and the dark ocean, scattered palely with luminous, moving scuts of white, was quite flat.

I dropped back and flung an arm across my eyes. I could hear the blood pounding in my ears, but the sound of the surf was just what was to be expected: the rising rush of an incoming breaker, the moment of silence while it hung suspended, its powerful neck curving in its descent, and then the uproar as it smashed on the beach. But it made an almost subdued uproar that bore no relation to the ominous thunder of my nightmare. All the same, what a fool I'd been even to think of sleeping on the beach, where the sound of the sea would be likely to bring it on.

I must go inland. But instead I lay there thinking: now that Professor Fairlie was gone there wasn't a soul I could talk to—and I didn't mean at length, but just enough to ease the pressure. I thought of Beth. Yes, there was Beth. And yet—she was involved with both Dad and me and somehow I wouldn't quite dare. She might, in her good common sense, convince me of something I didn't want to be convinced of. Who then?

Dunstan. Big, quiet, wounded Dunstan, someone entirely separate, of another world, as Professor Fairlie had been and who, no doubt, had had his own nightmares. "*God,* but kids can be cruel!" And maybe it hadn't been only the kids who'd been cruel.

I looked across at the island, but there were no lights. Everyone had gone to bed. And I turned over and closed my eyes to think about Dunstan—and slept until morning.

Two evenings later, "—And imagine having dreams like that, time after time, and then being stupid enough to sleep on the beach!"

Dunstan smiled his slow, thoughtful smile.

It was now six, and he had closed half an hour ago, having gone outside to take in a trough of books and seen me coming along the High Street. "Andrew! And here I thought never to set eyes on you again! I thought you'd be on your way back to the States by now. Come and have dinner with me."

So off we went and I told him about the walk to the

sea, and about the nightmares; so then, of course, I told him the whole thing—that is, just to do with Hoagy.

He asked no questions, but simply listened in his open, receptive way. And finally, after the slow smile, while he looked into his cup and then up at me, "But you didn't have the nightmare when you slept by the sea, nor did you last night. And you've been alone for five days and four nights, actually, except for the times when you've asked people the way and bought food. You've been alone with your own thoughts and come through safe. And that's something, isn't it?"

So then Dunstan understood exactly how it was with me. "Come through safe," he'd said. And meant that perhaps this hike alone, having been spent for the most part in a state of vegetable content and at times of positive exhilaration ("I felt so good the whole way, Dunstan—I felt so damned good!") proved I was OK after all. And maybe, even, that I might never have the nightmare again if even the sound of the sea in my ears the whole night hadn't brought it on.

I told Dunstan about my mother's book arriving, and what kind of book it was, about the quotes on the jacket, and that there was to be a publisher's party that I had to go home early for.

"Will it be a very posh party?"

"Oh, I s'pose so. But then, I don't know, never having been to one. I don't want to go. I'll feel like a damned fool and out of place—why should *I* be there? I won't know a single person, and what'll I say to anybody, and what'll anybody say to me? 'Well, young man, and what do you think of your mother's book?' 'Don't know. Can't read it.' End of conversation. I don't know why she wants me there. To show the family, I guess—a piece of it anyway. My father won't be going. I'd a million times rather stay here."

I sat there thinking of the long journey home and after that the party to be gotten through. And I told Dunstan about wanting to go to school and work for the McBrides evenings—live there at Cames and have that room up at the top that used to be Dad's. That was the room I wanted, I knew all at once, though I hadn't known it before, and not because it had been Dad's, but because of its height, like an eagle's eyrie looking out over everything: the loch, the hills to the south in front of Cames and out into the west. Sometimes, Jim said, you could make out the minuscule train creeping through them on its way down to England. If I couldn't stay now, at least I could have that room next summer.

"And after three more years of school," I said, "I want to go to St. Andrews."

Dunstan was astonished. "But, why, when you have so many universities in the States? What put that idea into your head?"

"Because I like Scotland, and because a friend of mine was determined to go there. I wonder if she ever did." I looked at my watch—I had to leave. And when I got up,

"Write and tell me about the party, will you?" said Dunstan. "It'll give you something to do—watching and listening and taking notes to yourself. It'll be amusing for you to write about and for me to read."

Amusing, yes. But I thought he hadn't meant just that. He'd meant food for dreams.

On the way back to his shop, I got to telling Dun-

179

stan about bouldering, the art of rock-climbing that you get into before you're ready for the big ascents, when you practice handholds and how to place your feet, and about managing cracks and crevasses and transverses, and how to use your head to save yourself.

"Is this what you want to do, Andrew? Climb?"

I wanted to see the world hiking, I said, and I wanted to go on bouldering, but not to get ready for going up the walls of Yosemite like Hoagy had wanted to do. Tis-sa-ack, the toughest climb on Half Dome, that's what he'd had in mind. But I'd never wanted that, at least so far I hadn't, standing on an inch of ledge, hanging by my fingernails over a mile of space between me and the bottom of the valley, staring out sideways across a cliff of smooth, merciless rock face with not a hold in sight. That was for Hoagy. He'd been preparing for Tis-sa-ack when he was called for Vietnam, and already his hands had begun to have the battered look of a climber's, though his weren't as bad as some, with the nails broken to stubs and the fingers and knuckles blackened with bruises.

And it was just then, when I was telling Dunstan about Yosemite, about Half Dome and El Capitan and the Cathedral Spires and how the falls thunder in spring after a heavy winter and how the family had always spent vacations there and in the high country, camping, when Hoagy and I were kids, that I thought of Bob Hoskinson and Buck Mathis and Phil Barnett. Those were the ones I'd sent postcards to, the fellows I'd been bouldering with before Hoagy was killed. And now, for the first time, the thought came to me

180

that perhaps it might be a good thing I was going back, for the reason that maybe it wouldn't be easy for me to make friends at school now the way it used to be, not in a country I knew nothing about. I'd known those three fellows so long, and just right then I had this little sudden feeling about wanting to see them again. I had so much to catch up on.

Dunstan lived over his shop and wanted me to come up, but I said no, I had to get on back. And we were standing there at the entrance when here came a girl, walking fast, with her hair swinging around her shoulders—very good to look at, and I watched her as she went by. And when she'd passed I glanced at him and he was still looking after her. Then he turned and saw my grin and laughed.

"A stunner, wasn't she?"

"Yes," I said, wondering if he had ever loved a woman and what had happened. "Thanks for everything, Dunstan." I held out my hand, and saw his eyes resting on me with affection. "I'll get along now."

"Safe home, then. And you'll write."

"Oh, yes. You can count on it—I'll write." And I set off down the High Street, turned and waved once, and saw him go in. Come through safe, he'd said. Maybe going to be OK after all, was what he'd made me feel. Oh, God—oh, thank you!

I was whistling as I went along toward the fields, and still whistling as I turned onto the footpath I'd taken the first time that led down over the hills towards Cames.

CHAPTER

23

It wasn't conceivable that that broad, sparkling beach, arched over by the brilliant sky, the green breakers rolling in with the sun glistening on their backs, and the turnstones and sandpipers flying up in a cloud as Hoagy and I ran toward them, could all be transformed so quickly.

Yet there it came—the gray nothingness sweeping in from the sea, and I heard the swelling thunder of the tidal wave even before I could see it coming. The broad beach narrowed to a dim, constricted prison, and Hoagy and I were caught and going down. I could hear Hoagy calling, but even as my body knew it must give up and the bitter water filled my mouth, I thought that at least if I went down, this would be the last time and I would never have to suffer this slow misery again. I tried to let myself go, but instinctively struggled, and after a timeless agony of choking, the waves threw me on the beach. I looked up—and there lay the familiar figure sprawled on the sand. Then the dead lips spoke, just as always, quite clearly though softly in my ear, as if the words were whispered, and I heard, though the figure lay some distance away, "You've won, Durry, but you've lost—won but lost." And I woke asking, how can a dead man speak, and *what have I won?*

I sat in the dark, on the side of my bed, listening to my father breathing, peacefully and quietly. My throat ached as if it had been burned so that I knew I must have been shouting in my sleep—inside my dream, because I hadn't waked him. I got up and made my way to the door, hesitantly, for fear of stumbling against something, making some clumsy move, and went into the bathroom to splash cold water in my face as I always did to bring myself out of the aftermath.

I stood there in the dark hall, trying to clear my mind, knowing I could not go back into that bedroom. I would get dressed and go out and walk; I would leave a note.

Instead I went along the hall and downstairs to the big room, and sat down and looked out over the loch to where, on the far side, lay the few scattered lights of Burney. I thought of Professor Fairlie and all there was still to tell him. I sat for perhaps half an hour or more, going over and over everything that had happened to me within the past few weeks, searching for some pattern, or meaning, or the connecting thread that I remembered Fairlie had thought was there. But turn the kaleidoscope as I would, no pattern or meaning revealed itself, though it would have—I was sure it would—if only Fairlie were putting his questions, apparently at random and yet one somehow leading to another and bringing facets to my mind that I'd forgotten, or pointing out those I couldn't see for myself.

Then I knew I was sick of the whole thing—I had a revulsion—and remembered Professor Fairlie saying, "You must never work at it—" and something about relaxed expectancy. So I lay down and pulled one of the big loose pillows under my head, curled up and closed my eyes, and labored at refusing to think.

But someone was crying. I opened my eyes to find the early light of morning making a pale oblong of the big window opposite me and couldn't imagine what had happened that it should be there. Why was I facing the window when my bed was turned away from it, and why was I cold and without blankets, and why should a woman be crying in this bedroom? I lay there listening and remembered coming down-stairs, and so decided it must be Beth. Yet why should Beth be in here at this hour instead of upstairs with Jim—and why should she cry?

Next, I knew that it was not Beth because my blood had quickened in the way I recognized and I was conscious of the familiar tingling all through my body. I listened—listened—but now the crying had stopped, and I thought it was over, whatever I might have heard. Yet I couldn't mistake this preternatural awareness, which continued, as if some connection were still to be made. I waited, my breath coming fast and light, as though my whole body were listening.

"—If only I had sent something, Barty, some word. It needn't have been this letter—"

"But why didn't you send it? It's a good letter—"

"No, no, it's not a good letter. I knew it the instant I'd read it through. If only I hadn't written the postscript, as though I were putting the Reverend Lowther's insufferable proposal beside Andrew's. You see that, Barty—"

"Ye-es. Yes, I do see it—"

"And I was only wanting to tell him everything, enjoying my character sketch of Lowther, getting more pleasure out of it as I went along, filling in every detail. Then it turned out to be cheap in a way that would have hurt him, worse than he'd already been hurt, as if I were denigrating him and his wanting to marry me. Pairing my rejection of him with my rejection of Lowther! And I kept thinking I would write the letter over—or just that part, but for some reason I didn't, and I can't explain. I don't know—I kept putting it off, thinking I had plenty of time. But I didn't. And he's dead, without a word from me—"

"And there's nothing you can do, Deedee. It's over—"

"Yes. And why do we fail those we love in these unexplainable ways? The guilt will always be there—"

Oh, I was sick!

"The guilt will always be there—" *But guilt about what?* God! And abruptly I got up and went to the window, and with that movement the voices ceased and I heard the silence singing in my ears. I was dizzy with nausea—I wanted to vomit, and went out to the loo in the hall, but try as I would, I could not. I leaned against the wall, lost in the depths of my sickness as I had been once before—but where? Yes, in the shop in

Glensburgh with Beth. What had happened? She'd asked, handing me her car keys, if I would go and get the van for her, because she'd bought too much stuff to carry that far. At once the awful surge of misery had heaved up. And then Beth caught herself: but of course I wouldn't have a license to drive. What she meant was, I was too young to have a license anywhere. I was fifteen. And I'd wanted to be sick all over the floor. But, why? *Why?*

I stayed there in the loo until I was sure I wouldn't lose control, then went upstairs, got my clothes from the bedroom, dressed, and went down again and outside. The sickness had abated a little but I still felt "gone"—and not only that but hideously depressed, as I'd been with Beth.

I'd walk—I'd walk it off. The morning was cool and fresh and fragrant with the early smells of pungent leaves whose pungency is increased by the night damp. I took long breaths and headed around the back of Cames, past the greenhouse, and down the steps to the lane. Why that way? Because of my mother. She'd said once that when she was blocked and could go no further, she would work with her hands: clean the house, clean out a cupboard, go into the garden and dig. She had no need to make a blank of her mind; it would go blank as far as her writing was concerned with the settling to manual work, taken up only with the little routines of lifting objects, digging, clearing out dead leaves, pulling weeds, cutting back vines. And gradually, as routine took over, the unconscious would begin sending up illuminations, rising like bubbles to the surface of simmering water.

I was headed for the wall, that particular section of wall with the break in it, just up beyond the gate at the end of the lane that I'd noticed the first time I went into the hills. I'd thought there might come a time when I could test myself, try mending that wall from what I'd learned on the plane. I would kneel there, studying the stones that had fallen away to see if I could decide where they belonged, and perhaps the old man would help me with those words to Deirdre that I still remembered.

I climbed and knelt at the break and began picking up stones, feeling their shapes in my hands, studying the outline of the break and testing one stone and then another, building up the outer wall—because that had to go up first, to a height of two feet, before I could fill in the heart stones and put on the through band; then build up again for two feet with more heart stones inside, and then the cover stone with the coping stones on top. But it was hard. I was the rankest possible amateur, and only rarely could I find a stone to fit exactly as it should in the place I wanted it to fit. Perhaps some of the stones had been carried away. But it didn't matter, I told myself. It mattered only that I was working with my hands, with the greatest concentration, choosing, testing, dropping this stone and picking up another.

Until I lifted my head and took a deep breath, because all at once I was hearing myself as I walked along the loch road in the dark, in that green dusk of the huge winds the night I'd seen Deirdre, when I'd been shouting, "What have I done, Hoagy—tell me, for God's sake, what have I done?" But I had no idea what I'd meant calling out those words in between making up the speech I should have made to that son of a bitch in the drawing room at Cames.

But I had done *something*—I was guilty of *something* in connection with Hoagy. Beth handed me the keys to the van and I'd gotten sick the first time. And now—oh, *yes, yes, yes!* "Go and get the van, will you, Andrew?" That was Beth. And "You drive—be all right, Durry—" That was Hoagy. Then I'd said—I'd said—and the sickness heaved up again and I knelt at the wall, bent over, with my face in my hands. Because there it was—what I'd said.

I remembered everything.

We'd been arguing. Or, rather, I'd been trying to persuade Hoagy to get out and go down with Tory. "It's the leg, isn't it, Hoagy? Hurting—"

"Paining like hell. It's sickening. It goes on and on."

"Can't you take more Perc?"

"Already taken too much—have to take more and more all the time, and more does less and less." And I remembered someone telling me once about Percodan, how you couldn't get a rush, you couldn't get wiped out unless you took twenty at once. Twelve a day and you were on your way. But it wouldn't be worth living like that. I didn't dare ask Hoagy how many he'd taken. "You drive, Durry," he said. "Better if you drive." He sat leaning over with his head on his hands that were locked together on the wheel.

"But I can't drive on a road like this. It's pitch black and the road is so winding and narrow with those awful drops at the side. I'd run us off. I can drive on the straight in the daylight, but not up here. Not now. Let's go down with Tory. Please, Hoagy—"

He was silent for a time, his head still on his hands. Then, "Can't do that," he said. "She doesn't understand about the Perc. Thinks there must be some other way. Besides, we'd only have to come up and get the car later. You drive—be all right, Durry—"

"No, no, it won't be all right. I'd get us into an accident and I haven't got a license. I'd likely kill us both."

Hoagy raised his head and spoke quite clearly, after giving a little laugh. "Well, I can't have you killing us both. OK, old man. You've always been a wise old man and you always will be a wise old man. But I don't want you going down with me—nope, nope, you go and get in Tory's car."

"But, Hoagy, please—"

"I'll manage. You'll see. I'll manage. Go on, now—"

And so I'd gotten out of his car and gone slowly over to Tory's. And we'd started off and then I heard the gunning of Hoagy's engine behind us.

Afterwards there was the knowledge buried away deep inside me of what I'd done—though I hadn't realized all through the time of not knowing what I could do with myself, or where to turn, or how I was to go on, what it was I was suffering from besides grief. Because the guilt itself had worked to conceal what Hoagy and I had talked about: that he had asked me to drive and I'd refused, and because of my refusal, Hoagy had gone down alone. How subtly our dreams express what is deepest: both of us had gone down, but only one had survived. As in the sea, so on the mountainside.

CHAPTER

24

The morning I was to leave, Deirdre's letter was in my inside jacket pocket, and *Animal Stories* and Donne's *Collected Poems* were in the small bag I'd take on the plane.

I went downstairs and saw Dad and Jim at the door, talking. Where was Beth? I went into the passageway leading up to her rooms and glanced into the kitchen as I passed. Not there. So I went on up and knocked on the half-open door. "Beth? I have to go—I want to say good-bye."

"Oh, Andrew, I'm in here, in the bedroom. Come in, dear—I've been hunting out some photographs to give you. Some of the castle in the early days. I'd have thought she'd want them—your Great-aunt Millicent—but, no, there they were amongst the rubbish. I think she must have given up at the last—too much to be dealt with. You know how it is. When you're dead tired, you either throw everything away or shove it all back in the box again."

I went into the bedroom and there was Beth, her face flushed with hurry, down on her knees burrowing in the bottom of a chest of drawers. "Why on ear-rth I would have left this to the last minute, I cannot say. I remembered them last night and should have dug them out then. Here they are." She got up and came to show me. "See, this large one is Great-aunt Millicent with all the aunts and uncles and the children round about her out on the grounds. One of those boys'll be your father, I'll wager. Let's see if we can pick him out—no, it's hard to tell. Won't he be surprised to see it! And you can get an idea of how fine the grounds were then, with the flower beds and the trees and the lawns. And then, here, these others are various members of the family, I suppose. Maybe your father can name them for you." She looked up at me. "Would you like to have them, Andrew?"

"Yes, I would. Thank you, Beth." I searched the faces, but of course Deirdre wouldn't be there. These were all taken too late. But still, wouldn't she have been alive, she and Barty? Why not? Perhaps I didn't recognize her as an older woman, or maybe they weren't at the castle, for some reason, yet wouldn't it have been her home?

"What is it, Andrew? Are you hunting for someone in particular?"

"Oh, I just wondered—" And I turned to Beth, standing at my side, and looked up and saw her—saw Deirdre, just beyond, a large portrait of her hanging on the wall to my left between two windows. The flesh crinkled down the backs of my arms—that sudden uncanny chill—and my expression must have changed because Beth at once turned to look where I was looking.

"Is it someone you recognize?"

What a shock, seeing Deirdre so unexpectedly, studying me with that frank and level gaze. "Yes, I think so—" Her hair was done up, rather high, and there was a sheen where it coiled around her head. Something silky was lying around her shoulders, leaving her neck and much of her shoulders bare, as if she were ready for a party. But why do I put it in the past tense? There she is, still looking out at me from her portrait, hanging on the wall opposite my desk here in my room at St. Andrews. She wears no jewelry, which is right for Deirdre. The portrait is in pale colors, possibly so as not to take the attention. You aren't even aware of them at first, the whole effect is so natural. I went toward her and, yes, her eyes were gray green, just as I'd thought they'd be.

"D'you recognize her from a picture at home? She's one of the earlier Mrs. Cameses. Mrs. Bothwell Cames—"

"Bothwell?" Again I suffered a shock. She couldn't have married someone else. Not possibly. No one but Barty.

"Yes, at least so it says on the back." Beth took down the picture and turned it over, and there, written in ink on the brown paper in a faded hand, was the name, "Mrs. Barton Cames."

I let out my breath. I couldn't have imagined how relieved I'd be that it was Barty after all. "Oh, Barton, of course," Beth said. "But how did you—?" Then didn't finish. They belonged together, those

192

two, I was thinking; they always had. It would have been unthinkable for her to have married anyone else.

"But I don't find this Mrs. Cames in the photo of the whole family." I said.

"No, because she died in London in her early forties. She'd lived there for some time, your Aunt Millicent told me when she decided to leave the portrait here. Her husband was killed in the First World War—such a pity they couldn't have had their lives together. She's quite beautiful, isn't she? Perhaps not beautiful in the usual way, but somehow there's something about her you wouldn't forget. Perhaps it's the look in her eyes." We studied the portrait in silence and then Beth said quietly, "Andrew, would you like to have it? After all, she's one of your forebears, and I think it belongs to you. I've kept it where it's always hung because the face fascinates me. I like to look at her. But I want you to have it."

I couldn't meet Beth's eyes and I had no idea what to say. What must she be thinking? Why, she must wonder, would a boy my age be so drawn to this portrait of a woman he'd never known? But she understood—I hadn't a doubt of it, even though she might be unable to be exact as to the details of what she understood. And she asked no questions; or only, did I want it?

"Yes," I said after a little, "yes, Beth—thanks, I would like to have it. I guess she'd be my great-great-aunt, wouldn't she? And Dad's great-aunt, like Aunt Millicent. How'll I get it home, do you suppose? Carry it separately? I hope I won't drop it." I was thinking how awkward it would be, and that I didn't want everyone on the train and in stations looking at

Deirdre and maybe asking questions. And what would Dad say? But I didn't care. I *would* take the picture.

"We'll pack it in your suitcase! I bet it'll just fit— come on, let's see." Excited, Beth hurried ahead. "Your bags are in the hall, are they, Andrew?"

We ran downstairs, I, clutching the photographs and the portrait under one arm, and just as we got into the little hall, there was Dad at the door at the end.

"Andrew!" he said, and he seemed enormously annoyed. "Good Lord, I've been looking all over for you. What have you two been up to? We've got to go—the train leaves in an hour. What's that you've got there? You're not *taking* it, are you?"

"Well, yes—"

"It's one of his great-aunts, and I thought he should have it," said Beth quickly, and she took the pictures from me and laid them on top of my suitcase. The portrait looked as if it might just fit, with no room to spare. I opened the lid, got down and took out some of my clothing, all carelessly packed, laid everything in, and pushed the clothes back on top. Of course the lid wouldn't close.

"This is crazy, Andrew! Why drag home a big picture like that? It'll be sure to get broken, the way they throw the luggage."

"But I want it. I'll get it packed all right. Why don't you go down and get the car started and I'll be right there, this minute. If it won't go in, I'll leave it."

Dad shook his head, gave Beth a baffled look, and turned away. "Can't imagine," he said. "A portrait of his aunt!" He went off along the hall and out the

194

door, and we heard him exclaiming to Jim, and after a while the car started up. We were kneeling together, Beth and I, and she took the pictures, cleverly and quickly refolded my clothes, and while she was rearranging them around the portrait, I told her about wanting to come back next summer to work and live there, and maybe every summer until I was ready for St. Andrews. Did she like the idea? Would they have work for me?

She looked up in astonishment. "Why, Andrew, of course! Why, we'd love to have you, Jim and I. I think it's a splendid idea." She was doing the top layer, trying to get everything as flat as possible. "And what does your dad say?"

"I know what he thinks—a kid's notion."

I was watching Deirdre's picture being covered with my things, and I imagined Bob and the others when they saw it hanging on my wall—they'd known my room for so long. "Who's *she?* Where'd *she* come from?"

Now the lid went down as it should and I could lock it. I got up with my two bags and we went together out onto the porch and saw Jim leaning in at the open window of the car on the near side.

"But, Andrew," and Beth put her hand on my arm, "never trust that everything will be the same, because it won't. You mustn't wait all year for what can't—"

"But *why* can't it? Cames'll be here, and you and Jim—"

"Oh, Andrew, you know I don't mean that. Of course we will, looking forward to seeing you again and having a bite in front of the fire and talking so

195

easily and comfortably as if you were our son. But it's not that. I don't know what's happened while you've been here and I'll never ask. But Cames'll be so different for you in another year. You might not even like it because your needs will have changed—"

"But *I* won't—I'll be myself—"

"Yes, always, underneath, the same Andrew. But this old place won't seem nearly so necessary. In fact, it may seem utterly boring, stuck out here in the hills, and working isn't the same as staying and doing as you please."

No, but it wasn't possible I wouldn't need to be here. I couldn't bear to think it would become unnecessary. Or—could it be it was Deirdre alone who was making me want to come back? Yet who knew if I would ever see her or hear her again, and why did I feel as I stood there with Beth that I probably never would?

Now there were two sharp blasts of the horn, and Beth put her hands on my shoulders and drew me to her. She gave me a kiss and I brushed her cheek with my lips, then ran down the steps. Jim took my bags and stowed them away in the back of the car, clapped me on the shoulder and wished me a safe journey. And I got in, and Dad and I were off down the drive between the two steep embankments, then out onto the loch road.

"Well," he said after a silence, "I suppose Beth got that picture packed up after all. I thought you were never coming."

"I was just telling her about coming back next summer, about working and living at Cames—"

"And what do you want to bet you won't see it that way next year?"

There it was again. "But why *shouldn't* I?" and I could feel my sadness and resentment mingled. "Didn't you always look forward to coming back? What's the difference?"

"Oh, Andrew—what's the difference! What can Cames mean to you after these few weeks? It was my other home for three months out of the year, year after year. And it was beautiful then. You can't imagine how it was. You can't begin to know the Cames I knew and what it meant to me. Now, here we are—" he said, because we were at the bend in the road where it curved south. "Look back, Andy! This is it, the last chance. It's where I always used to look back at the end of every summer."

I turned and saw mist drifting thickly across the sun, blurring the towers and chimneys of Cames, making them indistinct, scarcely to be seen. A moment longer and even as I watched they were blotted out entirely. I turned back and Dad said something, but I didn't hear. I was seeing the ruin of stones in the hills and Deirdre walking with her easy stride down among the black Angus, and heard her singing to herself that Gaelic song in a minor key that, even so, was not sad.